MEL TORREFRANCA

MAELIN

Lost Island
PRESS

MEL TORREFRANCA

MAELIN

A BELLADONNA NOVELLA

Lost Island
PRESS

Maelin
Copyright © 2024 Mel Torrefranca

Library of Congress Control Number: 2024907462

ISBN 978-1-962876-03-2 (paperback)
ISBN 978-1-962876-02-5 (ebook)

Cover illustration by Natalia Orshulevich
Select interior illustrations by Gonzalo Mansilla

Lost Island Press LLC
Oro Valley, AZ
lostislandpress.com

GUARDIAN DIVISIONS

RESEARCH

DEFENSE

MEDICAL

I never met my cousin, but I will never forget her
May we watch the night sky and remember

For Jennifer

INTRODUCTION

Maelin wasn't supposed to exist.

After publishing the first book in the *Belladonna* series, *Nightshade Academy*, I dove straight into writing the second one, but the idea of this companion novella wouldn't stop pestering me. I eventually accepted that I couldn't *not* write it.

So I put *Underground Royalty* on hold, and here we are.

Maelin is told through the eyes of Blimmery, my favorite instructor in *Nightshade Academy*. He's a charismatic guardian in his early fifties, a warm light in the cold Force. However, as the plot unfolds, readers learn that behind his laughter lies a heavy burden.

When Blimmery was twenty-two years old, he wrote a false article for the press about how his fellow guardian Maelin died. His lingering remorse for doing so compels him to prevent Yahshi—an Academy trainee who thinks like Maelin—from suffering the same fate as her.

Perhaps you're wondering why I'd write this novella, considering how *Nightshade Academy* exposes the ending. What more is there to tell?

Well, quite a lot, actually.

The idea struck me in the summer of 2023, soon before *Nightshade Academy*'s publication. I was tweaking Chapter 25, in which Yahshi reads about Maelin in the archives. *What if Blimmery did more than write a lie about her death?* I wondered. *What if he was involved in the events leading up to it?*

From those questions arose *Maelin*, which dives even deeper into Blimmery's past. While the history uncovered in *Nightshade Academy* is indeed the truth, it's only a morsel of it.

The first challenge of writing this book was fleshing out how and why Blimmery gets involved in Maelin's death. The story underwent multiple iterations before I settled on the version you're about to read. I'm glad I integrated Blimmery's disgraced family and his passion for writing into the central conflict.

The next challenge was defining Blimmery and Maelin's relationship. I knew they would graduate together, but I didn't know how close they should be. My initial plan was to mirror their bond with Yahshi and Vell's, but after some thought, that choice felt trite. Of course the ending would be tragic if Maelin died as Blimmery's best friend!

I wanted a fresh direction that would require pushing my creative boundaries to land the ending with a solid punch. *Would it be more intriguing,* I asked myself, *if Blimmery was an acquaintance instead of a friend? An outsider looking in? A third wheel, perhaps?*

The answer was an electrifying *yes.* I loved the idea of Blimmery caring about Maelin without being her *bestie.* And that's where Taig came in.

Writing Taig's dynamic with *Mae* and his verbal jabs at *Blim Blim* left me laughing alone in my pitch black apartment night after night. *Maelin* is the first book where I encouraged myself to be as silly as possible, and I hope it shows.

What began as an opportunity to purge a pesky idea out of my system turned into a book that I spent hundreds of hours on over the course of four months. I'm talking tears, laughter, and lattes—the full deal.

Don't be fooled—*Maelin* is not a spinoff but a tale woven tightly into the *Belladonna* series. While you don't have to read this novella to understand the main books, or vice versa, I planted Easter eggs and cross-references for the enjoyment of those who do.

Maelin has been loads of fun, but I'm ready to grieve the loss of a story

I love—and let it go. So, without further ado, I invite you to turn the page and travel thirty-six years before *Nightshade Academy*, to when Blimmery was not yet an instructor, but a trainee himself.

I'll regroup with you in the acknowledgments. Until then, this story is Blimmery's to tell.

MEL TORREFRANCA

CHIANG MAI, THAILAND · MARCH 23, 2024

PRELUDE

If you're reading this book, I must be dead.

If I'm not, I will be soon, because this story exposes what the Force ordered me to cover up. It's the truth about Maelin Vandros, a girl who graduated from Belladonna Guardian Academy beside me and died four years later.

I wrote a beautiful lie about her, and I fear that if I don't write the ugly truth to counter it, I'll lose my sense of what actually happened. So despite the risk, and the knowledge that my words may never see the light of day, I bring my pen to the page for my own clarity, and to pay tribute to a noble soul taken too young.

My name is Blimmery Owding, and I dug Maelin's grave.

The boy woke within the confines of four towering stone walls, instinctively rising to his feet. There was no ceiling, nor a sky. Just a hole into oblivion. Even his own name was a mystery. All he knew was that he was no longer *home*—whatever that meant.

THE WALLWALKER

BLIMMERY OWDING

IGNORANCE

CHAPTER 1

TRAINEES

The boy scraped his fingers along the cold stone walls,
cursing them for sealing away a world just beyond reach.

♫ NERVOUS - OLIVER RIOT ♫

Two months into the program at Belladonna Guardian Academy, a field class exercise sent us into the woods to extract willow bark, a medicinal pain reliever. While I scanned the trees for slender trunks and drooping branches —hallmarks of willows—a flapping noise caught my attention.

In the distance, Maelin pinned a crow to the dirt as it tried to fly away. "Please, stay with me..."

Taig knelt, casting a shadow across Maelin's face. "If an animal's dying, it's meant to die, Mae. Circle of life. Leave it be."

I frowned at his curt tone, creeping closer. Since our first day of training, Taig had clung to Maelin like moss to a log, and her laughter always coaxed out his smiles. *I thought their harmony unshakable.*

As I neared, a gust of wind plucked flowers from their stems, tangling blossoms into Maelin's hair. It was like nature itself was saying, *Take these pretty pink petals, Mae. They belong to you.*

The crow didn't seem to think she deserved them. It squawked and flickered its wings, splattering blood across the white sleeves of her button-down.

I halted, gagging at the sight of a gash in the bird's chest.

Taig's voice was deeper now. "It lost too much blood."

After a moment of thought, Maelin sighed. "You're right."

My eyes widened as she snatched a rock and raised it over the crow's head.

"Wait!" I shouted, stomping forward.

Her hand paused mid-air, and she looked over at me with a tight-lipped grin.

"Turn around, Blim Blim," Taig said, a hint of humor in his tone. "City brats can't handle pain."

Ignoring him, I held my gaze on Maelin.

"I promise, Blimmery, I tried to save it, but I was too late." Her grip on the rock tightened. "Now it can only suffer to the end, so isn't it kinder to let it go?"

The crow went quiet, its beak opening and closing as it struggled to breathe, either due to Maelin's suffocating grip or its leaking wound. I wasn't sure.

But she's right. It's suffering.

I nodded and flinched as Maelin swung the rock down.

It turned out that Taig was right too. A City boy like me couldn't handle pain.

If there was one person we *knew* would make the final five, it was Taig Bitterview. The sixteen-year-old was designed to become a guardian in the Force. With the build, the brains, and the smile as intimidating as it was captivating, everyone wanted a piece of Taig. Everyone wanted to *be* Taig. It was always Taig, Taig, Taig.

So naturally, I couldn't stand him.

I can't say he didn't intrigue me though, especially after Maelin killed that crow. *Why is a predictable boy like him best friends with a fiery girl like her?* Their dynamic was a jigsaw puzzle I felt called to finish. The closest thing I had to a best friend was Cove Starfall, but she was no longer with me.

It was Taig's mysterious bond to Maelin that significantly limited my interactions with her at the Academy. In fact, I only spoke one-on-one with her four times during our eighteen months in the program, the first taking place about a month after the willow bark extraction exercise.

Six minutes until class, I noted, eyeing a clock on the vine-covered wall. The Medical lab, located on the highest Academy floor, resembled a conservatory more than a room of instruction. Being alone under its dome-shaped glass ceiling, surrounded by plants overflowing their pots, always put me in a writing mood.

I plopped my notebook onto a standing lab table. *The Wallwalker* was a fantasy novel about a boy who could—you guessed it—walk through walls. If my family name weren't soiled, perhaps I would have been able to publish it someday.

Quite foolish of me. I plucked a pen from my book bag. Any distraction from the program would threaten my chance of making the final five. To win would not only earn me a respectable job as one of a hundred guardians in the Vakoi Empire's Force but would also clean the mess Uncle Meridian had made. *I should be grateful and focused.*

I was one of twenty promising fifteen- and sixteen-year-olds offered a trainee contract, and among us, only the best would graduate, the losers weeded out through intellectual, physical, and emotional testing. One trainee fainted nineteen times before filtering himself, begging to go home while a pack of boys laughed in his face. Soon after, the only other girl besides Maelin sabotaged her own Research exam, seeking a less humiliating escape. Our number dropped to fourteen in just three months.

But even with the boarding school demanding my absolute dedication, I couldn't stop squeezing words into the brief moments I had to breathe. Creating a world where I controlled everything kept me sane in a world where I had little control over anything at all.

The door creaked open, stealing my eyes from the page. It was the first time I saw Maelin enter a room without Taig at her side.

She scowled as she hurried down the aisle. "Wondering where Taig is?"

I hesitated. "Not really."

Maelin crouched by a potted belladonna plant growing in the shade of a chamomile bush. "Apparently, he thinks I raise too many questions during Research class." She scoffed. "As if the Empire forbids *learning*!"

I tensed up when she lifted the pot, half-expecting her to chuck it across the lab.

But instead, Maelin exhaled, and her voice softened. "You're not getting enough sun, are you?" She spoke to the plant with genuine concern, like she'd spoken to the injured crow.

My shoulders loosened. I started to wonder if she was kinder than I thought. Hell, I started to wonder if she was kinder than me. *Because if I had been the one to find that crow, I would have let it bleed out and die.*

"There." She placed the pot in a beam of light. "Much better, don't you think?"

I closed my notebook. She heard the pages clap and looked back at me, her sharp eyes pressing for words.

"Umm..." I panicked and said the first thing that came to mind. "You know that belladonna won't talk back, right?"

"How would *you* know?" Maelin stood and dusted her pants. "Belladonna's really quiet, and you're not a good listener."

My lips twitched, suppressing a smile. *How could Taig's sidekick have a sense of humor?*

"Well, I might not talk to you much, but I do listen. I actually consider words my strong suit."

"Of course you do, Blimmery. But you're a writer, and writers are notoriously bad listeners, despite what they claim."

"If you're so confident in your listening skills," I countered, strolling toward her, "why don't you tell me what your dear friend is saying?"

Maelin leaned over, squinting at the plant's dark purple berries. Even when I stopped beside her, and the door welcomed a few chattering trainees into the room, she held her concentration.

"Hey!" Maelin snapped, making me flinch. "I know Blimmery can't hear you, but that's just cruel!"

A chuckle escaped me. "What did it say?"

"I'd rather not repeat it."

"Why?"

"It's foul."

"Damn." I knelt and flicked a belladonna leaf. "Quite a feisty little thing."

Another voice cut into our conversation. "Not everything's a joke, Blim Blim."

My smile vanished. Taig was the only person who called me that. *Blim* sounded like a word to describe the slimy bits of a rotting fruit.

"If you're so interested in plants, why don't you become an Imperial gardener back home? You could tend to the Prince's tulips."

"Taig..." Maelin warned.

I stood, facing him with a forced grin. "Relax, Bitterview."

"Your uniform buys nothing." Taig poked a four-petaled flower button on my vest like it was stupid—like his uniform wasn't identical to mine. "City folk don't need your community infrastructure bonus. Their buildings reach the clouds already."

"That's an exaggeration," I muttered.

"And I doubt, even more, that your family pension goes appreciated. What is it to them? Coins on the gold bar? An extra ticket to the art gallery?"

"You're asking *me*?" I faked a confused look. "I just play my violin while the butler cooks me supper. What do I know about money and government?"

Taig leaned in. "No one needs you here."

"If anyone's unneeded here, it's you."

"You're wrong. *I* need me here because unlike you, I don't have a ritzy family to console me if I lose."

I lost myself in his eyes, my mind racing with memories of my parents flipping through bills they could no longer afford, classmates questioning me about my uncle's execution, and my little brother crying over bullies calling him *Mini Meridian*.

"You know nothing about my family," I said, raising my voice. "If I lose, they won't console me. They need this win."

Taig paused, his eyes widening. "You're here because of the boycott."

I pursed my lips. He was right, *again*. If Uncle Meridian hadn't written that treasonous book, I wouldn't have signed the trainee contract. I'd be at home instead, agonizing over my failed writing projects, rebuking my brother's gripes about trivial matters, and rolling my eyes at my parents' disapproving remarks. I'd be dealing with problems better than Taig.

"You're only here for show!" he exclaimed, taking my silence as confirmation.

"So what if he is?" Maelin asked. "He was selected for the program all the same."

Taig faced Maelin, and his crumbling smile raised my brows. The pair spent so much time together that if one of them were to jump off a cliff, the other would've followed suit. *But I'm learning they agree on less than it seems.*

I patted Taig's shoulder. "Well, I guess I'll leave you and your lovebird —I mean, *birdlover*—alone."

Maelin laughed when he shook my hand off, his face reddening.

"Oh, and Maelin," I added. "You should move the belladonna back. It won't grow as many berries in direct sunlight."

"Okay, *Doctor*," she teased.

Taig yelled at me as I walked away. "Can't wait to see you hop, Blim!"

The hop. Oh, how I dreaded the hop...

Commander Blank had informed us that in two weeks, we'd have to jump over a bar to keep our spots in the program. Thanks to the advanced notice, I could hardly work on *The Wallwalker*. Almost every time I'd open my notebook, a nagging voice in the back of my head would say, *You shouldn't write, Blimmery. Put the pen down and hop, hop, hop.*

"Level one!" announced my roommate, Wick Saratoga. He arranged our pillows on the forest floor, then pointed to a tree branch. "Jump over that, and land on this little cloud here. Easy pie!"

Wick had offered to help me train in exchange for studying assistance after overhearing me recite a scene from my notebook one night. According to him, I could read faster aloud than he could read mentally. *"Not everyone comes from a lineage of authors like you, Blimmery."*

Following Wick's instructions, I sprinted into a jump and spun so my back faced the branch.

"Too low!" Wick shouted.

The branch caught my vest, halting me and breaking under my weight. It struck the ground before I plummeted and slammed onto it, missing the pillows.

"Agh! It hurts!" I cried out, rolling off the branch and clutching different parts of my back. "I broke something! I broke—"

Wick burst into laughter. "Aww, do you need your diaper changed?"

"Help me," I croaked, struggling to push myself up.

"Boys!" Professor Dealio's roaring voice rustled leaves in the woods, his black boots snapping twigs with every step toward us. "What the hell are you doing?"

Wick stood tall and cleared his throat, cutting his laughter off. "We're training for the hop, Professor."

Despite my aching back, I scrambled to my feet.

"You call this *training*? Disrespecting Imperial property?" He grabbed the branch I'd broken and whacked my shoulder with it.

I shut my eyes with a wince. "Sorry, Professor."

"Was this Saratoga's idea, or yours?"

I slowly opened my eyes, and the middle-aged guardian tossed the branch aside, his face red, his gaze unblinking.

"Mine," I lied.

He gritted his teeth, unsheathing one of his back-strapped swords.

Before I could think to run, Wick shoved me off my feet, and I hit the ground screaming. The edge of a log scraped my arm, drawing blood, as Wick shielded his face from the oncoming strike.

I shot up into a seated position. "No!"

As the plea left my mouth, Professor Dealio pivoted, striking our pillows instead of Wick. His belladonna-laced blade sent a cloud of dove feathers into the air, turning my vision white.

"No supper this week for either of you!"

Ten days later, I gazed up at the raised bar in the training room. It was higher than Wick had prepared me for. Impossibly high. And according to Commander Blank, we would have one chance to scale it, a hop that could make or break our entire futures.

Kanter stepped forward. "I'll go first."

Despite being antisocial, Kanter sure wasn't afraid of taking initiative. He had been the first volunteer to drink belladonna-laced beet juice, the first to race Taig for a Defense exercise, and the first to poison a rabbit with serum in the lab.

"He's going home today," whispered Wick.

I nodded. Kanter Lorain was the anti-Taig, the boy who *wouldn't* make the final five. Because no matter how much initiative he had, he was still scrawny, which made him look weak, and reserved, which made him look vapid. He resembled the trainees who slipped a little more each day until they snapped under the pressure and went home in shame.

But I hoped he would prove us wrong. It would make for a good story.

The lone wolf, I mentally narrated as Kanter positioned himself a fair distance from the bar. *With everyone betting against him, he wins with nothing but the fire of his spirit!*

Trainees gasped as Kanter shot off into a leap. He soared over the bar with an elegant spin, and his shaggy hair rippled upon his descent.

I smiled when he plopped onto the beanbag.

"Maybe tomorrow," Wick said.

Next up was Taig, who glared at the bar while he stretched his hamstrings.

Maelin shoved her way to the front of the spectators, folding her hands together.

Why is she worried? Taig had passed every filtration effortlessly so far. *He's incapable of failure.*

Proving my point, Taig ran into a jump, scaling the bar with more room to spare than Kanter. His vest and button-down flew up for a second, allowing me a glimpse of a burn on his abdomen.

With a satisfying *plunk*, he landed on the beanbag. A few trainees cheered for him. Others scoffed because they *weren't* him.

Taig smirked as he pushed himself to his feet.

"Extraordinary," Commander Blank said.

Wick nudged my arm. "I bet you can do better." He spoke so loudly that eyes turned my way.

I shook my head, half to argue against his claim and half as a request for him to *shut it*.

Wick didn't get the latter message. "Oh, you can, you can! I know it!" He cupped his palms around his mouth and chanted, "Blimmery! Blimmery!"

A couple of boys joined in, so I had no choice but to smile and hide my desire to kill them.

Taig was rejoining the spectators when we crossed paths. He stopped me with a pat on my shoulder. "Time to hop, Blim."

My head spun as I readied my position. *Don't let his comment get to you*, I ordered myself, which backfired, because now I was thinking about Taig's comment more. Now it was looping in my head, over and over. *Time to hop, Blim. Time to hop.*

After a few deep breaths, I managed to clear my head.

"You've had enough time, Blimmery," Commander Blank warned.

I inhaled a deep breath and dashed forward, channeling my weight to my legs before launching into the air. The momentum wicked the sweat from my skin while I traveled high and far over the bar. So far I completely passed the beanbag.

I screeched, my ankle twisting as I crashed and rolled onto the black floor. A numbness prickled from my foot into my calf, leaving me grimacing to fend off tears.

"He should see Doctor Rem," Commander Blank decided.

"I can take him," offered Kanter.

"I'm already doing it," objected Wick. I couldn't help but cry out as he pulled me onto my good foot.

Commander Blank crossed his arms. "Hurry back."

"You think I'm that much of a cheat, huh, Commander?" Wick exchanged a smile with the guardian as he dragged me toward the exit. "Faster, Blimmery! Faster!"

I flinched with every step, and Maelin gulped as we passed her.

"Slow down," I whispered, my face warming up.

"Wow, you're really in pain, huh?" Wick clearly knew it but didn't seem to care. He laughed our entire way up the spiral staircase, recapping the hop from his perspective. "...And then you just *flew*, Blimmery! I bet you were up there for ten seconds or something. How'd you do it? Did you put springs in your boots? I mean, that wasn't even human."

Doctor Rem wrapped my ankle in the infirmary, a simple, cozy room across from the lab. Wick told him what happened three or four times, and the guardian never failed to burst into laughter during each retelling.

Behind my smile, my blood boiled. While their teasing wasn't a big deal, the pain in my ankle made me an oversensitive baby about it. *Just because I like to joke around doesn't mean I like being the joke.*

"You still have to hop," I reminded Wick, and he laughed even louder.

"Alright, I get it. I've annoyed you enough." Wick swiped an extra pillow from my infirmary bed and pouted at Doctor Rem. "Mind if I steal this?"

"Wick..." Doctor Rem warned.

He returned the pillow with a sigh and headed for the door.

"Wait," I called weakly.

Wick stopped to look back at me, brows raised.

"Give me a smile, Wick." I faked a sickly cough. "I want my last memory of you to be a happy one."

He shook his head, grinning. "Oh, shut it, Blimmery! I'm not getting filtered. Just you watch. In about ten minutes, I'll be up here with a broken leg, not a measly twisted ankle. Because I'll hop *that* high."

"Wick?" Doctor Rem said.

"Yeah?"

"Quit stalling."

"Fine..."

Doctor Rem waited until Wick shut the door before meeting my gaze. "Cheer up, kid. You jumped higher than Taig."

I smiled back, my ankle throbbing a bit less.

"You'll be as good as new in a couple of weeks, and we don't have any physical filtrations planned in the meantime, so you have nothing to worry about."

"No *physical* filtrations? Do elaborate."

"Nice try." Doctor Rem placed the bandage roll on my nightstand, preparing to leave. My aching body urged me to ask a question I had been wondering for weeks.

"Doctor?" My smile faded. "Does it hurt?"

He trailed his fingers along the branding on his forehead—a four-petaled flower, the same Academy emblem embroidered into our trainee uniforms. Every guardian had a permanent mark.

"Not anymore, Blimmery. Just at first." Doctor Rem patted my arm, and made his exit.

With no one to chat with and nothing to do, the pain consumed me. My only escape was through a nap, so I closed my eyes, hoping to drift off.

It was pointless. Sleep had never come easily to me.

I opened my eyes at the sound of a creaking door, expecting Wick—but it was Maelin who entered, mug in hand.

Why would she visit me? I rubbed my eyes, expecting Maelin to morph into Wick. *Was there serum in our juice today?* Hallucinations were a side effect of the belladonna doses mixed into our lunch juice, a measure ensuring that by graduation, the final five would be fully tolerant to the toxins lacing their tools.

"Surprised?" Maelin kicked the door shut behind her. "You thought I failed the hop, didn't you?"

It's really her.

I winced, shuffling into a seated position. "That's not it."

"I know. And don't worry—Wick passed too. We're down to twelve now." She walked over and offered the mug. "It's my own blend of willow bark, chamomile, and mint. Should help with the pain."

"I'm not in pain. That was nothing."

She laughed as I took the tea.

"Thanks," I added, raising the mug to my lips. The earthy bitterness of willow bark melded curiously with the floral chamomile and cooling mint.

Maelin pulled a chair to my bedside and took a seat. "I'm really sorry about Taig."

I chuckled, and a bit of tea dripped from my mouth into the mug. "What?"

"I know he's rude to you. He's not a fan of... you know..."

"No, actually. I *don't* know. Care to enlighten me?" I leaned toward her, eyes wide.

"He hates City folk."

"I don't blame him. I'm a spoiled, entitled City boy. I write fiction while people are starving on the streets. What's there not to hate?"

Maelin rolled her eyes, and a pang of guilt scared my smile away. Her effort to have a serious conversation was lost because of me. *Read the room, Blimmery.*

"He's too much though," she continued. "I mean, yes, Taig and I had a very different upbringing than yours, but—"

"Frontal Orphanage, right? I heard they beat the children there." I regretted the statement instantly.

"They didn't beat us."

"Sorry, I—"

"It's the children who beat each other."

I couldn't suppress my grin. "Really?"

"Why do you think Taig is so tough?"

With an amused nod, I took another sip. Then I remembered I had spit into the mug—which almost made me spit again—but I restrained myself and drank my own spit-tea like the rebel I was.

"I'm just here to make peace, Blimmery." Maelin leaned back in her chair. "Taig doesn't hate you. He just hates your history."

"Right. I don't hate mushrooms. I just hate how they taste."

She frowned at me, and I broke a grin.

"I appreciate your peace treaty, but relax. Taig is Taig." I shrugged. "I can handle him."

"But if he hadn't pestered you about the hop, you wouldn't have jumped that high and hurt your ankle."

"No. I still would've jumped that high."

Maelin smiled. "Oh really?"

"Oh, definitely. Taig doesn't deserve any credit. That was all me."

We talked a bit longer, and I remember feeling that she left me too soon.

CHAPTER 2

WINNERS

In his attempts to scale a wall, vines snapped and fingers slipped
until the boy collapsed onto the ground, bruised and defeated.

♫ MARS · SLEEPING AT LAST ♫

When my fellow trainees spoke of home, they mentioned people—parents, siblings, friends—who at this point, they had gone half a year without seeing. They wanted nothing more than to hear their voices, taste their dishes, feel their embraces...

There were people I missed. Cove Starfall, mainly. But I would be lying to say I missed people more than Vakoi City itself. I missed the vibrant paintings on the sides of buildings, the sound of music humming in all directions, and the coastal air breezing through my open window at night.

"Oh, quit playing special, Blimmery. You miss people all the same!" said Wick when I highlighted our differences. "You miss art class? No, you miss your classmates. You miss your family's home library? No, you miss the authors. And for the glory of Vakoi, you miss Cove's perfume? No, Blimmery, you miss Cove! Who *is* Cove?"

"Wick's right. You're just like the others," Taig butted in, stealing an empty chair at our dining table. "You miss home and wish you could return, while Mae and I hate home and wish never to return. If we fail, there's nothing good waiting for us."

"Home isn't rainbows and cookies for me either," I muttered.

"Oh, but it's sunshine and sprinkles, and that's close enough." Taig reached out and straightened my tie. "Don't forget that you're only here for show. My nightmare is your playground."

"What a victim!" Wick said.

"What a *Bitter*-view," I mocked, but Taig was right, as usual. I only signed the contract because it was my responsibility to do so, for my family.

"Blim Blim Owding, the Vakoi City Martyr," Taig mocked back. "Wow, what a bold sacrifice. Giving up your dreams as a book writer so people will buy your parents' stories again. What a hero."

"They're called authors, not book writers."

"Only book writers would care about the words that describe them."

I raised a brow. "Orphan."

"City slum," he hissed.

Wick laughed when I said, "Looks like we *all* care about titles, then."

I circled Wick, dagger in hand, sweat trickling down my forehead. The clinking of metal echoed in the training room as I blocked another attack. He was relentless, pushing me back with rapid strikes that left me wishing I wasn't too prideful to wear training armor.

"Stay guarded!" Wick said, his boot striking my stomach.

Despite scrambling for balance, my feet betrayed me. I collapsed onto the polished floor and groaned as my dagger skidded away.

Wick laughed and offered a hand. "Were you not listening?"

Rejecting his help, I pushed myself up and spotted Kanter leaning against the wall, watching us. A wall torch cast a menacing shadow across half of his face. *He's sizing up his competition*, I assumed, goosebumps dotting my arms. The more Kanter succeeded, proving us wrong, the more unpredictable and threatening he seemed.

"What are you mad at *me* for?" Wick said, stealing my attention back. Despite the twinge of humor in his tone, I could tell I'd offended him by not taking his hand.

"I'm not mad at you. I'm mad at the program." I picked up my dagger. The tool felt foreign in my grip, mocking my upbringing. It wasn't my fault I hadn't trained in combat before joining the Academy, or that I overreacted to pain because I'd never earned more than a bruised knee growing up.

"Be mad at the program all you want, but don't take it out on me. I'm the one helping you *beat* the program." Wick clapped once. "Now stop being a baby, and let's get to work!"

I strangled my dagger and stormed toward the nearest target. *If I can't land a shot this close, I'm not cut out for guardianship.*

With a sharp exhale, I swung my arm, chucking the tool across the room. The dagger spun violently and landed backward, its handle hitting the target's outer rim before clattering against the floor.

I huffed. "And throwing blades are supposed to be my strong suit."

"Yes, *throwing blades*." Wick's tone sharpened. "Stars and darts. Not daggers. You're not meant to throw daggers."

"Taig can throw daggers."

"Well, Taig is Taig. You know that."

I crossed my arms and frowned at my boots.

"They say trainees from the City are too soft to graduate, and you're proving their point."

"Maybe they're right," I grumbled.

"So why are you here then, huh?" Wick asked, raising his voice. "If you hate the program and think you're too soft to win, why don't you stop wasting my time and filter yourself already?"

My chest tightened. I had pushed Wick's buttons before, but never enough to make him snap. How careless it was for me to take his help for granted. Before enough trainees were filtered to allow us each our own living quarter, we had spent four months as roommates—and through our late-night conversations, we had become friends. Good friends. I should have appreciated him more than I did.

"I thought about filtering myself." I looked up at him, dropping my attitude. "Four months ago, when I had to use crutches after the hop."

"It was only a sprain."

"Exactly. It was only a sprain, but it hurt worse than anything I felt before." I wasn't raised to be strong and protect people. I was a *writer*, and a bad one, at that. If I couldn't complete a book from start to finish, how could I expect myself to see the Force's grueling program through to graduation?

"I'd rather be home," I continued, "but if I don't graduate, people will see through my publicity stunt. They'll realize I joined the Academy just to make my family look honorable. Graduating is the only way to prove, without a doubt, that my parents aren't treasonous like my uncle. It's the only way readers will trust them enough to buy their books again."

"And mommy and daddy will finally be proud of you?" Wick added smugly.

I turned away briefly, shaking my head.

"Don't get me wrong, Blimmery. I like having you around. But I know you're not doing this for you. You're doing this for them. And you don't owe them *anything*, okay? I say you go home now and finish *The Wall-walker*."

"I stopped working on it."

"Why?"

"You're not hearing me, Wick. If I go home, no one will buy my parents' books. And no one will buy mine either."

He went quiet, and I could tell by the look on his face that he finally understood my lose-lose situation. At least graduating would leave me with a secure career and the knowledge that I'd done something to help my family. I wouldn't be worthless.

After a moment, Wick said, "I never told you why I trained for my selection."

"I could never pry it out of you," I replied, raising a brow. Unlike me, who had stumbled into this opportunity thanks to high exam scores and experience in Vakoi City Secondary's slingshot troupe, Wick had intended to be here. He spent years improving his academic, athletic, and social skills

—all to make himself so impressive that the Academy guardians couldn't resist offering him a contract.

"The truth is, I'm a huge fan of your mother's fantasy books."

I tilted my head. "What?"

"The way she writes about the City... it makes you feel like you're there yourself."

I couldn't argue with him. Despite her characters being fictional, my mother hadn't glamorized her settings. They weren't based on Vakoi City. They *were* Vakoi City.

"I know it's superficial, but I only wanna be a guardian so I can live in the City myself someday. And I'd also love a shot at getting your mother's autograph."

"Even though she's an Owding?"

"I don't care about the Meridian book. That's on your uncle, not his family, and I can't be the only one who sees that. Readers won't boycott their stories forever. You don't need to be here. The storm will pass."

"Look, I appreciate the concern, but I'm doing this." I stepped toward him. "So you can either keep lecturing me, or you can help me train, and I'll see what I can do about that autograph."

Wick smiled. "Alright. As long as you're sure."

"Hey boys!" Taig shouted. "Are you done crying on each other's shoulders yet?"

We looked over to find Taig and Maelin by the door.

"How long have you two been there?" I asked, my cheeks hot.

"Long enough to feel pity." Taig held his hands up, which were shaking from our recent belladonna dose. "But don't flatter yourself. If the poison wasn't messing with my emotions, I wouldn't waste *any* sympathy on the likes of you."

"*Serum*," I corrected. "You know how Doctor Rem feels about that word."

"Poison, poison, poison!" Taig whined in a child-like voice.

Maelin picked up my dagger and studied its handle as she walked it back to me. "Why's it all beat up?"

"No reason." I snatched my tool without looking at her.

"Well, this has been fun," Wick interrupted, "but Blimmery and I are in the middle of a highly productive practice session. So, I'd like to politely say... Go away, Taig!"

"You don't have to say that twice." Taig headed for the door. "I wouldn't have come if I'd known that Blim Blim would be here."

"Go away, Taig! Go away, Taig!" Wick said in that same child-like voice.

I laughed. "He said it twice anyway!"

Taig ignored us, peering over his shoulder. "Come on, Mae."

"No," she said dryly. "Wick and Blimmery don't own the training room."

Taig narrowed his eyes, and Maelin stared back with equal intensity. To leave with him would be easy, but she chose to make a scene, to imply he was being a pushover. *Why is it such a big deal to her?*

After a moment, Taig broke eye contact. "Fine. But that's their side, and this is ours." He pointed left and right.

"Fine," Maelin echoed, heading for a tool cabinet in the corner.

"You hear that?" Taig asked Wick and me. "Stay on your side of the room."

Wick saluted him. "Your word is my command, sir."

"Don't talk like that," Taig said.

"Aargh!"

As Maelin grabbed a pair of daggers from the cabinet, her gaze drifted to Kanter, who was still leaning against the wall in observation. She took a deep breath before approaching him.

Kanter blinked when she asked, "Do you wanna join us?"

Despite his silence, Maelin grinned and offered him a dagger.

His lips parted slightly as he reached for the handle—but with a glance at Taig, he retracted his hand.

"I'd rather study," Kanter said in a monotone voice, fumbling through his book bag for a textbook.

He almost agreed, I noted. *What if he wasn't watching us to size up his competition?*

Maelin lingered by him for a moment before rejoining Taig with a glower. She clearly knew his facial expression had pressured Kanter into declining.

"Mae..." Taig said.

"Forget it." She handed him one dagger and raised the other. "Just show me that technique."

As they started to practice, I faced Wick in a fighting stance.

"Wow," he said, mirroring me. "I wonder what lifted your spirits."

"Shut it," I said, blocking an attack.

Our sparring match only lasted a few minutes before I was on the ground again. But this time, I took Wick's hand.

"Quick break," he said, pulling me up.

With a nod, my eyes found Taig across the room again. He was oddly patient, almost gentle with his movements, allowing Maelin time to react and learn. And every so often, he would smile and share a word of encouragement like *Nice one* or *Good, just like that*, and I couldn't help but feel that part of him was kind. Just not the part he showed to me.

Wick tracked my stare and chuckled. "We should convince them to filter themselves and get married."

I squinted. "Married?"

"Guardians aren't allowed to be in love, so it's a win-win. Saves their relationship and cuts down the competition. We'll go from ten to eight, just like *that*." He snapped his fingers.

"You're kidding, right? They're not... in love."

"You're just biased and don't wanna believe it." He elbowed my side, and I gently shoved him away.

"Stop that. It's obvious they're not."

"Oh, what do you know about love, Blimmery?"

"What do *you* know about love, Wick?"

"You think I was born this charming?" He stole my dagger. "Now dart time! Darts!"

We swapped our daggers for throwing blades, and it was nice not to feel skill-less for a change. My stars and darts hit the bullseye more than Wick's thanks to my time in the slingshot troupe. We had honed our aim for silly performances, not for combat, but it gave me an advantage nonetheless.

Wick didn't allow me to revel in being superior for too long. He threw a dart in the opposite direction.

"Hey!" Taig snapped. "This is *our* side."

Wick pointed to his boots, which were clearly on *our* side of the room. "I'm still following your rules."

"Your blades aren't."

"I didn't realize tools were subject to the rules... Ooh, that rhymed!"

I threw a dart next. It flew over Taig's shoulder and struck the target behind him.

"Let's practice outside, Mae," Taig said, scowling at me. "They might actually kill us."

"Don't be scared," I teased. "I didn't hit you, did I?"

"I could be standing a full forest away and I'd still worry about you hitting me."

"A full forest? You think my arm's that strong?" I laughed. "Thanks! I appreciate it!"

Wick threw another dart, purposefully hitting a mounted torch and dislodging it from the wall. Its flame extinguished against the floor as it rolled toward Taig's boots.

He backed away, his breaths quickening.

"Sorry," Wick said. "Maybe you're not safe here after all. I have *no* aim whatsoever. Such a klutz. Would you mind putting that back?"

Taig stared at the empty wall mount, his knees bending slightly. But then he looked down at his boots and took an extra step back.

"I'll get it." Kanter slammed his textbook shut, and I flinched. *I forgot he was still here.*

"No," Wick said, raising his palm. "I wanna see *him* do it."

Taig's face reddened as Wick scanned him in curiosity. "You're the one who dislodged it. Come over here and put it back yourself."

"Hmm..." Wick rubbed his chin. "You see, I would, but the rules force me to stay on *my* side."

"This is ridiculous," Maelin said, marching past Kanter and Taig. She grabbed the torch and used a lit one to reignite it.

"Thanks, Mae," Taig muttered.

With fire reflecting in her eyes, Maelin sent Wick and me a chilling glare.

The next morning, Professor Dealio passed out our graded essays. I received a solid ninety percent for my piece on our twelve-year-old Prince, who was expected to inherit his father's title as Emperor Vakoi in the next few decades. Hours of meticulous crafting and fine tuning had culminated into a final draft penned in flawless calligraphy.

I was proud of the score my hard work had earned—until the bell rang, and the lecture hall filled with rustling as trainees packed up.

"Bitterview," Professor Dealio called, "stay behind for a minute. Your essay was impressive, and I'd like to discuss it further."

My blood boiled as I jammed a textbook into my bag. *Writing is* my *thing.* Yet here was the star trainee, Taig Bitterview, impressing the never-impressed Professor Dealio.

"Cool down." Wick caught up to me as I stomped to the door. "Since when is Professor *Delirio* the benchmark of literary taste?"

"Just a *hint* of recognition would be nice."

"External validation is loser fuel, Blimmery."

We entered the hallway after Maelin, who slowed to a stop to wait for Taig.

"Hey," Wick said as we headed to the staircase, "you know how guardians get to choose their own formal wear?"

"What about it?" I replied, looking over my shoulder at Maelin. *Why did she invite Kanter to train with her yesterday?*

"If I make the final five, I'm gonna request formal wear so ugly that everyone will look at me. Imagine the power of confusing an entire ballroom!"

"That sounds like a good plan," I said, disinterested. "I'll catch up in a minute."

"Don't kiss her."

"Wick!" I shoved his back as I turned around, heading the way we'd come.

Maelin chuckled as I approached her. "What do you want?"

"No small talk?"

"Life is short."

"Alright then." I leaned against the wall. "I-I just wanted to apologize for the torch thing. Wick and I weren't trying to piss you off."

She shrugged. "I'm sorry too."

Now I was the one to chuckle. "Why's that?"

"Ten trainees were filtered already. We're still here because we're more alike than different." She looked away, her smile fading. "If we had met anywhere else—anywhere but the Academy—maybe we all could have been friends."

I imagined myself being a friend of Taig's and cringed. "Not all of us."

"Well, I believe it. I think we'd all get along if it weren't for the program turning us against each other. Turning us weak."

"Weak? We train for *hours* every day. I'm finally gaining muscle. I'm getting stronger."

"And what are you losing?" she asked.

The lecture hall door swung open, and Taig stole our glances.

"Blim," he acknowledged, joining us in the hallway. That was all he had to say to imply my presence wasn't welcome.

"I'm just here to make peace, Taig." I shot Maelin a final look before walking toward the staircase alone, pondering her question.

What am I losing?

I knew becoming a guardian would mean losing my future as a writer. But I had never considered what I would lose on the inside.

I thought about her question for a long time. So long that I'm still thinking about it now.

Three months later, we gathered in the courtyard at dawn. My head ached from consecutive restless nights, my muscles cramped from hours of daily training, and my hands—covered in paper cuts—stung from study sessions under the candlelight.

"This is your final filtration," Commander Blank announced. "Congratulations on making it this far."

"Congratulate us when we win," Wick whispered.

Professor Dealio raised a palm. "Eight of you remain, but only five will stay for supper."

"How dramatic," I whispered, louder than Wick. Professor Dealio scowled at me, and I looked away, eyes wide. *Oops.*

Maelin snuck me a grin.

"In today's filtration, we'll be testing your speed and agility in a game of retrieval," Doctor Rem explained, gesturing to the field. Five golden trophies were scattered about the middle, and five pairs of flags were spaced evenly along the perimeter of the surrounding woods.

My stomach twisted into a knot. I had played retrieval countless times at Vakoi City Primary. Our instructor would blow their whistle, and we would race to snatch a cone and carry it through our safe zone. The caveat was that there were fewer cones than players, and the *leftovers*, as we called them, would have to set up the next round.

Except this time, at Belladonna Guardian Academy, the cones were trophies, retrieval was only to be played once, and the leftovers were to be sent home with their spots in the program revoked.

"Lorain," Professor Dealio said, "follow me to your safe zone."

Kanter stepped forward as Commander Blank called for Taig.

Maelin squeezed Taig's hand before he left her behind.

"Blimmery," Doctor Rem said, gesturing for me.

Wick patted my shoulder. "Good luck."

As the guardians led us to our designated safe zones, a few beams of sunlight broke through the clouds, illuminating the five golden trophies. The game hadn't started yet, and my pulse was already racing.

"Be speedy." Doctor Rem stopped at two indigo flags. "I'd rather not lose you."

I couldn't bring myself to smile back before he walked away. In all the games of retrieval I had played, I had always been a leftover.

This is my chance to undo your mess, Uncle Meridian. I positioned myself between the blue flags, my legs trembling. *Nine months of training, and it all comes down to this.*

Within a few minutes, all eight of us had been led to our safe zones, where we waited for Commander Blank to blow his whistle. Our eyes flew around like bees as we tried to anticipate who would rush to which trophy.

Running after one that no one else had targeted would be the best strategy, but with everyone theorizing and no one locking their eyes in confirmation, any attempt to plan ahead was futile.

I didn't flinch when the whistle finally pierced the air. Locking my eyes on the nearest trophy, my legs carried me faster than I'd ever run before. The field morphed into a blur of motion—all seven of my fellow trainees sprinting like their lives depended on it.

Eyes on the prize, I reminded myself. *Don't look anywhere else.*

I dove for the trophy as though it was a rabbit that could hop away at the last second. It was cold to the touch and weighed more than anticipated, which slowed me down as I stumbled to my feet and sprinted for my safe zone. A trainee who had targeted the same trophy pivoted toward a different one.

I sighed, thankful he hadn't tried to fight me for mine.

In my peripheral vision, Taig stumbled to a stop at the sight of Maelin running in the same direction. He headed for a different trophy, which another trainee was closer to. *He wants her to win so badly that he's willing to lose.*

Nearby, Kanter claimed a trophy and bolted for his black flags. A trainee in his path dodged him as though he were untouchable. He was the first to win, and he didn't even smile.

The sky darkened as soon-to-be-leftovers targeted the trophies in our hands. I ran in swirls, dodging their attempts to snatch my family's future. There were a few close calls, but I eventually ran between my indigo flags, winning the game for the first time.

I fell to the ground, my heart beating so quickly I feared it would burst. While I caught my breath, I scanned the field for Wick, who beat a trainee down until he was writhing, just to steal his trophy. Wick was more violent than necessary, but I didn't judge him for it.

The clouds darkened as Taig tackled the boy who had reached his targeted trophy first. They pulled on opposite ends in a tug of war.

Maelin darted between two boys who had been ganging up on her. One of them split off and went after Wick's recently stolen trophy instead. That's when I closed my eyes, unable to watch.

The field grew louder with scuffles and shouts, the noise reaching a peak when Commander Blank's whistle pierced the air again. Trainees stopped fighting and grunting and running.

It was quiet. The game was over.

Still, I didn't open my eyes. I wasn't ready to know if Wick, the best friend I never had in Vakoi City, would be forced to leave me. And despite my dislike of Taig, I found myself sympathizing with him for a change, because I knew he was right—there was nothing good for him back in Frontal.

It's for the same reason that I wanted Maelin to win, because if she were to get filtered, Taig would have nothing good for him here either.

It felt like an eternity passed before I forced my eyes open.

Kanter hugged his trophy as though he planned to never let it go.

Wick waved at me and chanted, "Final five, Blimmery! Five! Five!"

Taig had taken a beating but had clearly given out more—two leftovers pushed themselves to their feet, their faces dirtied.

Maelin, with a bleeding scratch across her face, dropped her trophy like it was worthless. She ran into Taig's arms, and he spun her around, laughing. "We did it, Mae!"

I looked down at my golden trophy. It was a rabbit with four-petaled flowers for eyes.

CHAPTER 3

SHADOWS

When the boy heard a cry from the other side, he reached out,
and in a breathless moment, his hand phased through a wall.

♫ I WISH I WAS THE MOON - EWAN J PHILLIPS ♫

With our five spots in the Force secured, the second half of the program
unfolded with a sense of liberation. Gone were the days of filtrations and
petty rivalries. Class time normally spent on lectures became periods of
self-study under the Academy guardians' guidance. They encouraged us
to hone our strengths and pursue our interests, a massive change after
spending nine months dwelling on our weaknesses.

The even bigger change, however, was the addition of monthly assignments to shadow guardians at work in Vakoi City, offering us a glimpse
into the lives we would soon undertake.

My shadow unit leader was a professor in the Research Division, which
initially disappointed me. While our official placements wouldn't be con-
firmed until graduation, the Academy guardians hinted that our shadow
unit's division indicated what they currently considered our best fit.

I hope the guardians change their minds and place me in Medical. I descended the staircase with my arms crossed, dreading my first shadow assignment. *I'd much rather share a division with Doctor Rem than Professor Dealio.*

Forcing my frown away, I entered the common room, where a guardian just a few years older than me was lying on a sofa, his boots propped on the armrest like he owned the place. My approaching footsteps distracted him from a book he was reading, which he closed and tucked into his overcoat.

"Good morning, Professor. I'm Blimmery, your shadow."

"The nephew." He hopped to his feet and squinted at me. "Treason, in the flesh…"

I chuckled nervously. "I-I promise I'm nothing like my uncle. He was a bad—"

"It was a joke." The guardian tucked his hands into his pockets. "The name is Ogga."

After a second, I broke a grin. Ogga's dyed hair was a wild shade of red, his untucked shirt poked out from under his armored vest, and his unfolded collars extended from his neck like miniature angel wings. He didn't act or look anything like the uptight Research guardian Professor Dealio's personality had framed me to expect.

"Hurry up." Ogga headed for the front door. "It's time to break you out of *Nightmare Academy.*"

"You didn't like your time here either?"

He laughed. "Who does?"

We made a half-hour horse ride to the Investigation Office, which was located just a ten-minute walk from my childhood home. Growing up, I had seen the guardian buildings but had never entered one. They were almost as sacred as Vakoi Palace itself, and on my first shadow assignment, I understood exactly why.

"Welcome to my humble abode, Shadow." Ogga waltzed into the common room with a swing in his step, his boots clomping against the marble floor.

I slowed, my eyes widening. Rows of bookshelves stretched toward the ceiling, hanging lanterns lighting their contents. And the windows, framed in gold and barred for protection, sparkled with stained glass and gems.

The Office common room was not of imprisonment, but of exclusivity.

"These books..." I gazed up at a bookshelf as I passed it. "Are they investigation transcripts? Journals of prior guardians or Royal Family members? There are so many!"

Ogga laughed. "They're just novels. Consider this floor the playroom. The real work is upstairs."

He led me to the archives on the second floor, and my jaw dropped. Hundreds of file cabinets. Bookshelves so tall they required ladders. Wooden desks of artistic craftsmanship.

It was in that mesmerizing room where I spent most of my time during shadow assignments, gathering and summarizing information to report to Ogga. Most of the cases I helped him with were related to the Atherus Empire, our less-prosperous neighboring land. It was home to a jealous faction called the Underground that had been crossing the border and causing havoc on our side of the island for the past seven years. The Vakoi Empire's Force had a responsibility to deal with the aftermath of their petty crimes, as Emperor Atherus did little to keep his own people in order.

Sometimes Ogga would send me hunting through the archives for old paperwork upon his indirect request.

"A group of five Underground rebels looted one of our town's markets late last year, but I can't recall the exact date..."

"This case reminds me of a vandalism incident five months ago, when the rebels painted a statue of Emperor Vakoi black. If only I could remember the name of the second witness..."

Ogga had a talent for requesting help in ways that made me *want* to help, rather than ordering me around, which he certainly could have done. He even showed me kindness when I made mistakes, which I appreciated, because I strangely made a lot of them.

"Hey, Shadow?" Ogga inquired during my second assignment. "Where are your notes from this morning's meeting?"

I stopped flipping through papers and looked up to see Ogga strolling into the archives.

"I left them on your desk, Professor, with that file you asked for."

"Are you sure?" He stopped and looked away, squinting as if recalling the memory. "I saw the file, but not your notes."

"Huh..." I frowned, wondering if the page had gotten lost in Ogga's disorganized desk. "Just a moment. I'll find them for you."

Leaving Ogga in the archives alone, I scaled the staircase to the third floor and searched through every page on his desk, and every file in his drawers. The notes I had taken that morning were nowhere to be found. *Where the hell did they go?*

After a second round of rummaging, I accepted defeat and made my way down the staircase.

Think, Blimmery. What did you write on those pages? Perhaps I could spare myself a scolding by rewriting the notes from memory.

Upon my return to the archives, Ogga was shuffling through files from the desk I'd been working at.

"Ah, look what I found." He held up the missing notes, then pointed to a stack of pages. "It was lost in this mess of yours."

I gulped, realizing my blunder. *I must have placed my meeting notes in the wrong file.*

"I'm sorry," I blurted, rushing toward him. "I didn't mean to—"

"Shadow!" Ogga snapped, leaving me frozen in my tracks. He laughed as he folded my notes along the creases—which hadn't been there that morning—and tucked them into his overcoat. "Don't worry about it, okay? I lose track of pages all the time. It seems I'm rubbing off on you already."

I sighed, a smile tugging at the corners of my lips. He hadn't made a fuss about my mistake—or struck me, as I was sure Professor Dealio would have.

"Thank you, Professor. It won't happen again."

Ogga patted my shoulder on his way out. "You're doing great."

I worked extra hard that day to make it up to him.

"Picture the Force like a body," Ogga told me once. "Research is the brain—professors run the system. Defense is the skull—commanders protect the system from danger. And Medical is the heart—doctors keep the system alive. Everything revolves around the Research Division, the genius of it all. The way I see it, professors make the rules."

I spent my assignments squeezing as many casual lectures out of Ogga as I could get. His confidence and ability to quote books on the fly made it hard to believe he could say anything wrong. He was the only person I had encountered who read as though it were essential to survive—as though written words were a necessity like food or water. I even heard that he entered the Office with a new book every morning, already finished with the last one. *If only I had his speed-reading abilities...*

The more time I spent with Ogga, the more he started to feel less like my shadow unit leader—my superior—and more like a friend. It's because of my growing comfort with him that I eventually worked up the courage to ask about his dyed hair and disheveled uniform.

"One of the Guardian Vows is to uphold a refined public image," I recalled. "Professor Dealio says that guardians are symbols of the Empire's glory, and it's important to look the part."

Ogga scoffed and shook his head. "No need to wiggle your words around. If you think I'm ugly, just come out and say it."

My blood ran cold. "Oh, I-I didn't mean—"

With a shove to my arm, he broke into laughter. "It was a joke!"

I sighed through a smile. *Thank the stars.*

"To answer your question," Ogga continued, "I look this way because I want to look this way."

"And the Force condones you for it?"

"Here's the thing, Shadow..." He grinned wider, leaning in. "Not every guardian can get away with what *I* get away with."

When I was a shadow, I liked Ogga. Only because I didn't know what else he was getting away with.

I always returned to the Academy from my monthly shadow assignments revitalized, memories of new meetings and chats with Ogga spinning through my head.

But Wick always returned with a pale face and a waning sense of humor, symptoms that would take a few days to pass.

The first time it happened, I didn't ask why. I couldn't forget the night many months prior when Wick had left our quarter to sleep on a common room sofa simply because I'd asked why he was crying.

I won't pry. I know how much he hates looking weak.

But the second time it happened, I couldn't help but cross that line. Wick hadn't taken a single bite of supper after his return, drawing stares from Maelin, Taig, and Kanter.

When I ran into Taig about an hour later, he asked me, genuinely, "Is Wick okay?"

While the five of us weren't all friends, we *were* all winners, and that commonality was enough to bring us a little closer.

"You didn't hear?" I replied. "Wick died ten minutes ago."

"Hilarious, Blim."

I faked a sobbing face. "It's not funny. He's gone."

Taig rolled his eyes and left.

I waited until I was alone with Wick in the training room that evening before asking the dreadful question.

"How was your assignment today?"

Wick practiced a dual sword sequence without looking at me. "You know I can't tell you," he said, referring to the shadow confidentiality rule.

"I know, but you seem off, and it happened last month too. Nothing bad is going on, right?"

"Blimmery," he warned, cutting the air with his blades.

"I'm sure Maelin and Taig tell each other about their assignments."

With a grunt, Wick chucked his swords away, and they clattered against the floor at my boots.

I stepped back, my eyes widening.

"Are you seriously trying to fool me into breaking the rules?" Wick swerved and finally made eye contact. "Because if you are, that makes you no better than your uncle!"

I'm only trying to help, I wanted to say, but his gritted teeth and heavy breaths muted me.

Wick turned around with a long exhale. "Sorry, Blimmery," he said in a soft voice, taking a few steps away. "I just... I get tired every now and then. We don't get many days off, and we've been here a long time. Almost a year."

I could tell he was lying, and as I lay in bed that night, I couldn't stop thinking about his swords clattering in front of me. The blankets weighed heavily on my chest, blocking my attempts to drift off. Even when I ripped them away, their ghostly pressure lingered.

I can't recall how much time passed before someone knocked on my door. I slipped out of bed to open it.

"Hi," Wick croaked, his eyes red. "Could—could you read me *The Wallwalker*?"

We sat beside each other on the floor, our backs against the wall, as I read my unfinished novel. I didn't ask him why he wanted to hear it, and frankly, I was too focused on cheering him up to care. I simply turned page after page until I reached the cliffhanger I never resolved, the ending that wasn't meant to be the end.

My heart skipped a beat. I had run out of words to comfort him, but in perfect timing, his head drooped onto my shoulder. He had fallen asleep.

We never spoke of that night again, but I would forever cherish the memory. It was my final tribute to a friendship on the cusp of its final chapter. It was the goodbye Wick deserved.

It's happening today.

My fellow trainees and I stood in the common room, where a gong, stove, and metal chair with locks and chains awaited us. I hugged my stomach, fighting the urge to run. Or vomit. Or both. The branding ceremony was an important milestone, a step toward becoming full-fledged guardians, but all I could think of was the pain I'd inevitably endure.

"Congratulations on one year in the program," Commander Blank said. "Today, you will finally earn your marks."

Doctor Rem raised a branding iron over the stove, and Taig stared at the four-petaled flower design on the end, which glowed ominously in the fire. He stepped toward Maelin, and she gripped his arm tightly, standing on her tiptoes to whisper something into his ear.

"Bitterview," Professor Dealio said, interrupting Maelin's message. "You're first."

Taig stiffened, and Maelin released his arm, stepping forward without missing a beat. "I'll go instead."

"No," Professor Dealio replied.

"What about me?" Kanter raised his hand. "I like going first."

"The order has already been decided," Commander Blank cut in. "Now, Professor Dealio called Taig first, so Taig will go first. Is that clear?"

Professor Dealio nodded at Commander Blank, thanking him for his intervention, before gesturing to the chair. "Bitterview, sit down."

With a gulp, Taig stepped forward. Maelin reached out for him but withdrew her hand at the last moment.

I made eye contact with Wick, and he forced a smile. "It'll be fine," he assured me. "An easy pie."

I couldn't help but notice the goosebumps on his arms.

When Taig sat in the metal chair, Commander Blank secured the locks that held his wrists, ankles, and neck in place. That's when reality struck, and he tugged against the restraints. I had never seen Taig so panicked before, and a faint voice in my head whispered, *Help him, Blimmery.* Which I ignored, of course.

"Please!" Taig yelled as Doctor Rem pulled the branding iron out of the fire. "I'll be a great guardian. I'll do everything right. Just please, don't mark me!"

"You need the mark," Doctor Rem said, approaching him.

"I don't!" Taig shouted, his eyes watering. "I don't! Please!"

"What the hell is wrong with him?" Wick whispered to me. That's when I remembered the scar on Taig's stomach, and the time he hesitated to pick up the torch. And now my eyes were watering too.

"I'll do anything!" Taig pleaded, his voice breaking.

Kanter grinned slightly, as though discovering Taig's weakness amused him. The perfect boy we knew melted right in front of us, but unlike Kanter, I wanted him back. Hearing someone as strong as Taig begging made my knees buckle. *If Taig can't be strong, how can I?*

"I said, let me go first!" Maelin said, storming toward the guardians.

Professor Dealio glared at Maelin over his shoulder. A chill ran down my spine at the memory of the pillow incident in the woods.

"Stay back, Maelin," Commander Blank warned, as though he were concerned too.

Maelin froze, her face bright red, her fists clenched at her sides. I feared that one more plea from Taig would make her snap. She would fight the guardians with everything she had, which would not be enough to hurt them. It would, however, be enough to hurt *her*.

Taig stopped shouting, realizing the same thing. "Please, Mae." His voice was quiet now. "Don't."

"Recite the Guardian Vows," Professor Dealio ordered, jumping on his moment of surrender.

Maelin shook her head as Taig complied.

"I-I vow to serve the Empire with absolute devotion," he muttered. "I vow to partake in Imperial ceremonies when called upon..."

Once Taig recited the twenty Vows we had memorized for Research class, Professor Dealio shoved a roll of fabric into his mouth.

"Bite it," he said, and Taig did.

Doctor Rem brought the branding iron closer to his forehead, and Taig closed his eyes, a whimper escaping the fabric in his mouth.

"No!" Maelin screamed, her voice so raspy that it sounded like a growl. She lunged after Taig, but Commander Blank's arms encircled her, hauling her back. Maelin kicked and struggled, her cries piercing the silence before Taig's muffled screams joined hers.

As the branding iron sunk into his skin, his eyes opened, and tears streamed down his cheeks. I hoped, for my own sake, that he was crying more than the pain justified.

When Maelin stopped struggling, Commander Blank released her, and she turned around, unable to watch Taig suffer any longer.

"He's gonna be okay," I said.

Her red eyes met mine in a whip. "Shut it, Blimmery! You don't know him!"

I closed my mouth, and she turned her back on me too, her shoulders shaking with silent sobs.

My forehead's itching and burning kept me awake for hours that night. I eventually gave up and headed to the common room.

I need fresh air...

The unbarred front door told me that someone had left the building first. I cracked it open to find Maelin sitting on the steps.

"Hi, Blimmery," she said, eyes on the stars. "You're still up?"

"No. I'm sleeping." I joined her outside and shut the door. "How did you know it was me?"

"You're the only other person who's ever awake this late," Maelin said. "I used to hear you through the wall, mumbling about your book in the middle of the night. What made you stop working on it?"

"Wow." I sat next to her. "I feel incredibly violated right now."

"It's not like I was trying to listen. And your voice was all muffled, so I couldn't make out the words, anyway."

I hesitated before asking, "What are you doing out here?"

She turned to me, revealing a swollen, red mark on her forehead. "I'm just thinking."

I cringed. *Is that what mine looks like too?* I hadn't the courage to face a mirror yet.

"Thinking about what?"

"Taig." Maelin returned her gaze to the stars. "They didn't let me go first."

"What do you mean?"

"The guardians," she said firmly. "Taig was upset, and I was willing to go first in his place, but they wouldn't let me."

"You heard Commander Blank. The order was already decided."

"Well, it's *their rules*, Blimmery! They can change the order if they want to!"

"Quiet," I snapped, peering back at the front door. The guardian quarters were in the basement, right under the common room.

Maelin shook her head with a scoff, but thankfully, she lowered her voice. "You would think they'd catch on to the fact that Taig's afraid of getting burned, and they'd let me go first, to ease up on him a little."

"The guardians never go easy on us."

"I'm not saying they should have *gone easy on him*. I'm saying they should have been kinder to a boy who's been nothing but their star trainee."

I traced her gaze to the sky. "Why *is* Taig afraid of getting burned?"

She didn't answer, and although I wanted to pry, doing so with Wick had never gone well, so I glued my mouth shut and stared at the moon with her. I remember thinking that, despite the circumstances, it was nice to sit with Maelin without Taig around. How selfish I was, to be thinking like that, when it was Taig she was worried about.

Looking back on it, I wish I realized that she was diving down a dark rabbit hole. I wish I said, *Listen to me, Maelin. You can't act like this. We're in too deep now, so you need to pretend that you trust the Force, and that guardians always do the right thing. You need to play the game until it's safe not to.*

I wish I knew that I could have saved her.

Well, I suppose there's no way of knowing whether she would have listened to me. But I wish I *tried* to save her.

I wish I knew that in just five years, she was going to die.

CHAPTER 4

GRADUATES

With restored determination, the boy stepped through a wall,
leaving his confines to enter a world brimming with possibilities.

♫ GOD OF DEATH · SUSTO ♫

With our graduation around the corner, the Academy guardians summoned a pair of fashion designers from Vakoi City, one of whom was, shockingly, my—

"Cousin!" Cove exclaimed as she charged across the common room. A few rainbow-dyed feathers on her dress weren't attached properly, and they flickered free, forcing her design partner to rush in zig-zags to snatch them from the air behind her.

I nearly toppled over when Cove skidded to a stop, her arms enveloping me. My nose wrinkled at the overpowering lavender scent, but I rested my chin on her shoulder and closed my eyes anyway. *How I've missed that perfume...*

It was hard to believe Cove Starfall was nineteen now, not the seventeen-year-old I had left behind. While I had been training at the Academy, she had graduated from Vakoi City Secondary to secure her dream job as a fashion designer. I had never truly processed that off the grounds, people were aging and going about their lives as usual.

"Cousin Blimmery, you little cutie, you!" Cove pulled away and shook me by my upper arms. "Oh, you're so fit now! You *must* tell my nutritionist what they've been feeding you!"

She looked out of place at the Academy with her jewel-decorated cheeks and puffy hair—both of which were hot fashion statements among City women her age. I nearly laughed as I imagined how my fellow trainees would react to her neon pink lipstick, but then I remembered that they were right behind me. Cove's appearance hinted at a past they couldn't relate to, and the branding on my forehead—which she was pretending not to notice— hinted at a past *she* couldn't relate to.

I looked away, my smile fading. I was no longer the overenthusiastic sixteen-year-old who ran circles around her, spouting out book ideas while she cut up fabric, pretending to listen. *Mhmm, Cousin. Sounds good, Cousin,* Cove would say. I knew she never listened, but I didn't care. I never entertained her extravagant clothing and hairstyle experiments either. Our bond grew through shared passion, not shared hobbies. We were both dreamers. *But I gave up on my dream a long time ago.*

"Nutritionist?" Wick whispered behind me.

"They study food, I think," Maelin whispered back.

Taig scoffed and likely withheld a snarky comment because Cove was present. I imagined how he'd taunt me later. *Wow, Blim Blim. Your cousin's made of feathers. No wonder you vomited when Mae killed that crow.*

We took turns sitting alone with Cove and her design partner in the dining hall to share our formal wear ideas. I requested a navy-blue suit with striped pockets and a polka-dot tie. The whimsical pop of colors and shapes was a nod to the illogical fashion I had grown up around.

Cove's face lit up as she scribbled my request. "Stripes and dots, like the City boy you are, Cousin!"

My session was over before I knew it, and I hesitated to leave. It was unfair of me to have an early reunion with Cove while my fellow trainees would have to wait until after graduation to see their families. I should have returned to the common room with haste, grateful for what little I could get. But I couldn't help it. I wanted more.

"I've missed you," Cove said, breaking the silence. I knew she said those sappy words just so I'd know it was okay to talk.

"I know you have," I replied, and she laughed.

"You should have seen me after you left. I was furious at your parents for encouraging you to sign that contract."

"Well, what choice did I have? Whether I joined or not, I'd never be a writer anyway."

She smirked, pointing at me. "That's what I thought too, but then I realized something."

"What?"

"I have no clue how good your writing is, but I know *exactly* how passionate you are. That passion will draw people to your words, whether you're a guardian or not."

"Maybe." I looked away. "After I retire."

"Hey, hey!" she snapped. "Look at me."

I sighed as I met her gaze.

"Don't forget it's the Force that writes for *Capital Weekly.*"

My eyes widened, a nostalgic surge of energy coursing through me. I had never considered the possibility of working for the press. *Could I really be a guardian* and *a writer?*

"Just say thank you and leave already," Cove added. "Our final meeting is with Maelin, and you're keeping her waiting."

I broke a smile, the opportunity finally sinking in. "Thank you, Cousin."

Maelin and I swapped places, and I spent the duration of her meeting alone, circling the perimeter of the common room while I imagined what my life could look like after graduation. Becoming a guardian didn't need to be a sacrifice for my family anymore. I was doing this for them, but I could also do this for me. *My dream isn't crushed yet.*

After the final meeting ended, I stared through a front window, watching Cove and her design partner cross the vast Academy field. She had instilled in me a childish optimism that seventeen months of training had drilled out of me. My eyes watered, but I blinked the extra moisture away.

"Why does she get to fulfill her dream," Maelin said, appearing beside me, "while you're stuck here?"

"I don't think I mind being stuck here anymore."

"That's not an answer, Blimmery."

I chuckled. "Fine. If you really must know, her mother—my aunt—took her husband's family name when she married."

"So the bad publicity doesn't affect Cove?"

"She's not an Owding."

"But Meridian was her uncle too, right?"

"Doesn't matter. I'm the one with his name."

It was silent for a moment before I felt Maelin's eyes drift from the window to me. "It must be hard to have lost what she has. Harder than it is to have never had it."

I faced Maelin, and she grinned. It was the first time a trainee had acknowledged that my motivation to sign the contract was rooted in pain, even if it wasn't the same pain as theirs.

Why did you sign your contract, Maelin? Why did you train so hard for a spot among the winners? Are you here to escape the orphanage, stay with Taig, secure a wealthy future, or something else?

To this day, I can only theorize, because I didn't have time to ask.

"Mae!" Taig called, stomping down the staircase. "Let's practice!"

Maelin left me without missing a beat. "What are we practicing?"

"Primary tool drills," Taig replied.

I returned my gaze to the window right as Cove vanished into the surrounding woods.

"Oh, and Blim Blim! I didn't know your cousin was made of feathers! No wonder you vomited when Mae killed that crow!"

I smiled at the window.

The evening before graduation day, Doctor Rem led me into the lab. It had become my favorite room of instruction during my eighteen months in the program, and it occurred to me that this could be the last time I'd enter it. *Perhaps I'll miss some things about the Academy after all.*

Doctor Rem swiped a jar of seeds from his desk and stopped near the embedded planter, a pool-like area filled with dirt that sat even with the marble floor.

"How suspicious it is to be summoned here alone," I said. "Are you plotting to kill me?"

"Quite the opposite, actually." Doctor Rem passed me the jar. "I want you to give birth."

Through the glass, I studied the tree seeds. There were mainly willows, maples, and other deciduous types. A few fruit ones.

"Choose your pick." He pointed to the planter. We had only ever used it for growing medicinal herbs, belladonna, and calabar. Never before had we planted a tree.

I smiled. "What's going on?"

"Many years ago, I told myself I would allow my favorite trainee to plant a tree in this lab."

"You must have low standards."

"Pick a seed and plant it before I change my mind."

I laughed as I opened the jar. Sifting through my options, I settled on a cherry tree, simply because its flowers would look gorgeous during this time of year. Doctor Rem nodded in approval as he took his jar back.

I dug a shallow hole in the dirt, my hand tingling from remnants of dug-up belladonna roots. My skin would not form rashes, though. Thanks to our juice doses throughout the program, I had built a tolerance equivalent to that of a full-fledged guardian. I hadn't reacted to belladonna in months.

I dropped a cherry seed into the hole. "Doctor?"

"Yes, Blimmery?"

"What would it take to join the guardians who write for *Capital Weekly*?" I covered the seed with dirt, and looked up to find Doctor Rem grinning at me.

"I'll see what I can do."

I hopped to my feet. "It's *that* easy? I only had to ask?"

"Don't get ahead of yourself. I make no promise beyond trying. My word alone cannot decide your final placement."

His modest promise was more than enough for me. As I watered the seed, I smiled so much that my cheeks cramped up.

Doctor Rem placed a hand on my shoulder, and together we stared down at the planter, where several years from now, a cherry tree would grow to its full size.

"Now you have marked the Academy, Blimmery, just as the Academy has marked you. No matter where you are, a piece of you will always be here. This tree will grow and blossom, and one day it will shrivel up and die. But it will decompose in this very soil for the next one. It will never be gone."

Death sounded so beautiful when he said it like that.

My fellow trainees and I didn't see the formal wear Cove had designed until graduation day, when we traveled by horse-pulled vault to the Guardian Complex in Vakoi City. It was a tower-like building with fifteen floors of flats, and we would have the honor of living there for the next forty years of vowed service.

We brought our wooden boxes of formal wear to our flats on the highest floor, and an hour later, returned to the Complex common room to reveal the outfits we had requested.

Unfortunately, I had arrived at the first floor just after Taig, who sat comfortably on a sofa. He had chosen a sharp, charcoal-gray suit with a subtle pinstripe design. A pink flower peeked out of his breast pocket, and black feathers lined his tie.

"Just for you, Blim Blim," Taig said, flicking a feather.

It took a great deal of effort not to laugh, but it was worth it. I didn't want to give him the satisfaction of sharing an inside joke with me.

"I see your cousin set out to embarrass you," he added, clearly itching for a reaction.

I figured I should amuse him, considering the special occasion, so I glanced at my striped pockets and polka-dot tie. "It's just a bit of color here and there."

"Much more than a bit. I look at you, and I see a rainbow."

Kanter emerged from the staircase next, dressed in a dark, midnight-blue suit that seemed to change shades as he walked toward us.

"Shadowy and mysterious, like the man you are, Kanter," I said.

He smiled in response, which stunned me out of smiling back.

"Look at mine next, Blimmery! Me, me, me!" Wick yelled, running downstairs into the common room.

My jaw dropped. "No."

"Yes!"

"No."

"Yes, yes, yes!"

Wick had opted for a bright orange suit as hideous as he'd promised after Research class one day. *"If I make the final five, I'm gonna request formal wear so ugly that everyone will look at me. Imagine the power of confusing an entire ballroom!"*

I couldn't stop laughing.

"What's so funny?" Taig asked. "Wick looks awful!"

"It seems your master plan is working," I said to Wick.

Taig's face turned red. "What *master plan*?"

"Cute feathers, Taig." Wick flapped his arms. "Caw! Caw!"

Maelin entered last, wearing a flowing, dusty rose dress with matching flats. She hadn't styled her unruly hair, and I was glad she hadn't. It reminded me of our field classes, when her waves would catch flowers in the woods.

"Quite the dress. Looks like you're ready." I couldn't think of anything clever to say.

"No." Taig stood from the sofa, removed the pink flower from his breast pocket, and tucked it behind Maelin's ear. "Now she's ready."

I found it odd—how he seemed to read my mind like that.

Maelin chuckled. "You're acting like it's my wedding day."

"It's all of our wedding days." Taig gestured around our circle of five. "We're married to the Force now. We even made our Vows."

Everyone laughed. Even Kanter. Even me.

The ceremony took place in the Vakoi Palace ballroom. My fellow graduates and I formed a line on stage, followed by Commander Blank, Professor Dealio, and Doctor Rem. The band's opening number was a work of art that caused my shoulders to push back and my spine to straighten. It didn't make me feel prideful; it instilled pride within me.

When the song ended, the crowd of guardians and invited City folk applauded. I spotted Cove in a fuzzy violet dress and waved.

She waved back.

The Academy instructors made a shared speech about how proud they were of us. I hardly listened as I braced myself for the announcement of my official placement. While I still wanted to be in the Medical Division with Doctor Rem, after a great time shadowing Ogga, I didn't mind joining the Research Division either.

Anything but Defense. The thought of traveling on expeditions to trace, fight, and capture criminals had never appealed to me. I might even say the idea repelled me.

At last, the fateful moment arrived.

"Blimmery Owding of Vakoi City." Doctor Rem raised a division badge that matched the ones on his shoulders. "Welcome to Medical."

The crowd cheered as I walked over and took the badge. Doctor Rem stated my unit leader's name, and a group of three strangers in the crowd waved at me. Ogga and the other members of my shadow unit waved as well. I smiled grimly. I would miss taking meeting notes, shuffling through the archives, and absorbing Ogga's casual lectures.

"We have also assigned you as a member of the team at *Capital Weekly*," Doctor Rem added. "A special role for a special few."

My smile widened as the crowd cheered again. I had been clinging to the hope of writing articles thanks to Cove, and despite Doctor Rem's promise to try, I had assumed I might have to fight for the role after graduation. But everything had played out perfectly. The Force had offered me my dream on a silver platter.

Cove clapped her hands above her head, her smile even wider than mine.

I stepped back into line, and one by one, the next official division and unit placements were announced, each a different path, a different life through guardianship.

Maelin. Medical. I made eye contact with her and clapped. *Doctor Blimmery and Doctor Maelin. Who would have thought?*

Taig. Defense. *Not surprised.*

Wick. Defense. I glanced at him, and his lip twitched downward. Now wasn't the time to ask why. Maybe the time to ask was *never.*

Kanter. Research. The Academy guardians had placed him in my shadow unit, and I wondered if he would get along with Ogga as much as I did.

The formalities gave way to five guardians' retirement speeches, and lastly, to celebration. Music filled the air again as guardians and guests danced in a whirlwind of color. Professor Dealio had explained that the ball symbolized our transition from one phase of life to another. We were not to walk into it, but to dance, because this new life was beautiful, and we were to be thrilled for it.

Cove invited me to dance, and the soft fuzz of her dress against my hands eased my anxieties about my first day in service tomorrow. *I'll do just fine.*

"Hey. See that man over there?" Cove gestured with her eyes.

I saw him. He was just her type.

"Make sure he's not a guardian," I said, and with a spin, I let her go.

"Quiet!" she scolded.

As she walked toward the man, I joined Kanter, who was leaning against the wall with his arms crossed.

"Congratulations," Kanter said.

I frowned at the crowd, hesitant to look him in the eye. *He's never spoken to me first before.*

"Congratulations," I echoed, confusion seeping into my tone.

After a moment, Kanter stepped closer. "Blimmery?"

"Yes?"

He leaned in and whispered, "Do you think anyone would dance with me?"

I finally looked at him. "Not if you don't ask."

"That fashion designer didn't wait for you to ask."

"She's my cousin, remember?"

"Oh."

I narrowed my eyes. Kanter's lack of initiative didn't line up with the boy I thought he was. The only other time I had seen him hesitate like this was when Maelin had invited him to train with her and Taig. He had almost taken the dagger, only to pull his hand back.

My gaze softened as I recalled the memory. *He's more shy than he looks, and Maelin saw that long before me.*

"Why are you staring?" Kanter asked.

I faced the crowd again. "I'm not."

"Yes, you were."

My eyes accidentally found Maelin dancing with Taig in the distance. Call me cheesy, but I really was happy for them, and how they had managed to graduate together. *Their harmony might be shakable, but their bond definitely isn't.*

As the band transitioned to the next song, the duo slowed to a stop. I raised my brows as Maelin parted from Taig and approached me.

"May I have this dance?" She offered a hand.

"Don't tell me Maelin's your cousin too," Kanter muttered. His eyes widened when I stole his hand and placed it in Maelin's.

She winked at me before leading Kanter into the crowd, going along with my plan flawlessly. And from the sidelines alone, I burst into laughter, because boy, could Kanter dance!

"Hey Kanter!" Taig shouted. "Dance with her any longer and I'll cut off your legs!"

I looked over at Taig, and he smiled at me.

CHAPTER 5

GUARDIANS

As he walked through walls in his new world, the boy found that the most challenging barriers to cross were not of stones, but of hearts.

♫ SCARED OF YOU - BOBBY ♫

The door jingled as I entered Brackle Beans. It was a gentle evening, the sunset casting an orange glow through the shop's street-facing windows. The clinking of porcelain tea cups, resonating harp notes, and soft conversations brought an instant smile to my face.

A few customers bobbed their heads at me, respecting my uniform. I placed a hand on my heart and closed my eyes in exaggerated flattery.

"The usual, Doctor?" asked the brewer behind the counter. I didn't understand why she bothered to confirm. I had ordered peppermint tea with honey every day for the four years since graduation.

"I'm a man of habit," I replied, and with a smile, she reached for a jar of loose tea leaves.

I plopped my notebook onto my favorite table by the window, where I could glance at a bustling road of people walking and riding horses to my right, or a peaceful shop of potted plants and a harp player to my left—

depending on which I was in the mood for.

My task that day was to write an update on the upcoming summit between Emperor Vakoi and Emperor Atherus. The Underground rebels from our neighboring land had been causing us trouble for nearly twelve years now. Their crimes of looting and vandalism had escalated to drug smuggling and forged coin distribution to disrupt our economy. We were hoping the summit would encourage Emperor Atherus to finally take accountability for this problem, because if he didn't dissolve the rebels among his people, the Force would have to, and that wouldn't be pretty.

"Make the article optimistic," our lead editor, an older commander, had instructed me that morning. *"The severity of the Underground's disruptions are steadily increasing, so it's only a matter of time before they involve violence. We need our people to know that we're working to bring this conflict to an end, before it turns into a bloody war. You hear that, Blimmery? Optimism! That's your strong suit. That's why I'm assigning this article to you instead of Professor Punk Pants over here."*

I contemplated his instructions and jotted down, *Emperor Vakoi Works to Prevent Atherus War in Upcoming Summit.* No, that was too dry. Not enough optimism. I tried again. *Emperor Vakoi's Diplomacy Brings Atherus Conflict Toward a Peaceful Resolution.* Yes, much better.

The door jingled, and I looked up to see Maelin and Taig enter Brackle Beans, their eyes scanning the decorated room like newcomers. *I've never seen them here before.*

Customers glanced curiously at their back-strapped primary tools. Taig's dual swords and Maelin's bow and arrows were the latest editions from Vakoi City Hospital's tool crafting and development department. I had chosen not to adopt the new set of throwing stars and darts—their golden accents were too flashy for my liking.

Taig spotted me and glared at the door as though he were about to make a run for it, but before he could, Maelin caught my eye.

"Doctor!" she exclaimed, her voice cutting through the quiet hum of the tea shop.

"Doctor!" I called back. It was a little tradition of ours whenever we crossed paths in the Hospital, which wasn't often, as she worked on the higher floors.

Taig crossed his arms, lingering a few steps behind her.

"Are you busy?" Maelin asked.

"Not at all." I closed my notebook and gestured for her to join.

Maelin sat across from me at my table, followed by a reluctant Taig. The brewer arrived immediately after to deliver my tea cup and take their orders.

Once the three of us were alone, Maelin plucked an arrow from her quiver and spun it between her fingers. "You don't like the new toys, Blimmery?" she asked, scanning the bandolier across my chest.

"They're tools, not toys, Mae," Taig muttered.

"Whatever." Maelin stashed the arrow and smiled at me. "I dragged Taig here to break some news."

He rolled his eyes. "Are you sure we need Blim Blim to join us for the news-breaking?"

"What news?" I asked.

"I've been cleared for operations," she blurted.

I chuckled in disbelief. "So soon?"

Taig smiled too, his pride overpowering his discomfort with my presence. "An operator at twenty-one? Has that happened before?"

"Oh, a few times." Maelin waved her hand dismissively. "I'm not special. But I *am* excited."

Taig and I went back and forth, spouting out a billion different ways to congratulate her. The Hospital had a strict vetting process for allowing Medical guardians to operate on patients. I wasn't any closer to clearance than the recent seventeen-year-old Academy graduate I worked with in the basement lab, but I didn't mind. *My real work is with the press.*

"The older doctors must be kicking themselves for still working with me in the serum and remediation department," I said. "I bet it won't be long before you're promoted to unit leader."

Maelin laughed. "Okay, now the flattery has gone too far. I'm nowhere near a promotion, and there are far bigger accomplishments than earning clearance."

"Like what?" Taig argued. "Not many guardians are trusted to perform surgery so soon, but you're an operator now. There's nothing bigger than that."

"Of course there are things bigger than that." The humor in her voice slowly faded. "People are dying all over, Taig. Especially in towns further east, where there aren't good hospitals. You saw one, back in Frontal, when you got that—"

"Mae," Taig snapped, saying her name like a warning. He held a hand over his abdomen, his brows knitting together as he scanned the tea shop.

"What?" she replied, as though she knew exactly *what*.

Taig stared Maelin down until she broke eye contact, shaking her head. Even when the brewer returned to deliver their tea cups, neither of them said a word.

The breezy air in the shop thickened and weighed on my shoulders. *Is Taig sensitive about discussing his scar? Or is he upset that Maelin diminished the importance of working at Vakoi City Hospital?*

I cleared my throat and forced a cheerful tone. "Well, I suppose this calls for a celebration. What do you say, Taig? Drinks tonight at Vakoi Square?"

I set him up with a perfect opportunity to shoot me down. He could have said, *"I'd rather eat my own fingers, Blim Blim. I don't drink with City slum like you."* But instead of indulging himself, he stormed outside without a single sip.

I frowned at Maelin. "What was that about?"

"Nothing." She finally raised her tea cup. "Now, tell me about this new article of yours."

As I write this book, the selfish side of me wants to sugarcoat the story and say that Taig was the bad guy, and that he picked on *me*, not the other way around. But the truth is, I wasn't always the kindest to him. He started the fire, but I didn't have to fan the flames.

There was one moment, however, when I felt something close to love for him. Maybe love is too strong. Warmth, perhaps? Or maybe it had something to do with the Vow I made during the branding ceremony to support my fellow guardians. Maybe that was it—responsibility, not empathy. Either way, it resulted in a moment when I treated Taig more like he deserved to be treated.

I wish I had been nicer during the other times too.

The encounter took place about three months after Maelin's clearance. I sat in the Complex common room with a lantern one evening, working on *The Wallwalker*. I had dove back into it after my parents started making steady sales again. My master plan was to write novels in my free time and publish them upon retiring from the Force in one mega-publication.

I was clearly overestimating my abilities, because even after spending years on *The Wallwalker*, the story still wasn't done. I'd rewritten scenes, given characters new names, scrapped ideas and executed new ones, then scrapped those and changed the names all over again. But I never once felt myself getting closer to completion.

The front door swung open, breaking my attention as Taig rushed across the common room. He was almost to the staircase by the time I processed that he'd entered at all.

And then something odd happened, because I found myself running after him, leaving my notebook behind. He raced up the staircase faster than I could keep up, forcing me to shout.

"Taig! What's wrong?"

"Oh, what do *you* care, Blimmery!"

He had never called me Blimmery before. Never. Somehow, it felt more insulting than every time he had called me Blim Blim.

"Just tell me what happened!" I yelled in a breathless voice. My last four years at the Hospital hadn't been as physically demanding as the Academy program, and unlike Wick and Taig, I hadn't kept up with exercise in my free time. *I need to restore my stamina before the Force notices my laziness. I made a Vow to stay healthy, after all.*

Taig paused to stare down at me, and I caught a glimpse of a bruise on his cheek.

"I told her to stop!" he yelled.

I doubled over, gasping for air as he continued to run, his boots pounding against the steps. For a moment I thought he was talking about his unit member with the curly hair. But once his footsteps faded, I just *knew* he was talking about Maelin.

The next morning, I knocked on the door to Wick's flat, my eyelids heavier than usual.

Wick's face lit up instantly. "If it isn't the doctor, the writer, the hero! To what do I owe the honor?"

"Morning," I replied, not in the mood to match his enthusiasm. "Do you know what happened to Taig?"

His smile faded. "No. What happened?"

"That's what I'm asking you. I saw him last night with a bruise on his cheek. I thought you might've heard something during your shift."

"Actually, I wasn't at the Facility yesterday. Had a visitation right, so I traveled out to visit family."

"Oh, well that's nice. How are they?"

"My little brother got into a school fight. Lost three of his teeth."

I frowned. "Seriously?"

"No." Wick chuckled. "How bad is Taig's bruise?"

In perfect timing, Taig left his flat, revealing a purple patch on his cheek that had darkened overnight. He slammed the door behind him and rustled through his overcoat for his keys.

"What happened to your face?" Wick shouted across the hallway.

Taig ignored him, his hands shaking so much that the key slipped around the keyhole, refusing to enter. After a few more seconds of fidgeting, he kicked his door with a grunt and faced us, yelling, "Leave me alone!"

Wick and I glanced at each other as Taig stormed down the hallway, leaving his flat unlocked.

"He's more bitter than usual this morning," Wick said. "I bet his *wife* knows what happened."

I glanced at the door to Maelin's flat, and Wick walked over to knock on it.

No answer.

He knocked again, to no luck. "She must be at the Hospital."

The questions whirled through my head as I rode my horse to work that morning. *Did Maelin leave earlier than usual, or did she not spend the night in her flat? How did Taig get that bruise? What did he tell Maelin to stop doing?*

As soon as I arrived at Vakoi City Hospital, I tracked Maelin's unit down. "Where's Maelin?" I asked.

The three doctors looked at each other before one of them said, "She's not here."

But if she's not in her flat, and not at the Hospital, where else would she be? I wanted to ask, but her unit scattered before I could.

During my half-day shift that morning, I continually messed up the ratio for my batches of emergency neutralizer, forcing me to restart and waste enough calabar beans to warrant a scolding from my unit leader.

When it was time to prepare and deliver medicine to patients upstairs, I asked every doctor I ran into a question about Maelin, picking up pieces of the story, one at a time, through whispers in the bleak corridors.

"I heard they interrogated her at the Facility all night."

"There's talk that she's getting sent to correction."

"She'll probably take some time off service."

Correction? One of the Guardian Vows we had made was to accept mental and physical correction if necessary, but we had never learned what correction entailed—only that doing something disagreeable could lead to it.

"I heard mental correction is like therapy—those silly talking sessions City folk pay money for. Sorry. I keep forgetting you're City folk."

"One of your unit members was sent to correction a few years back because he wasn't taking his maintenance vials. Go ask him."

"It's true, but it wasn't a big deal. The corrector let me off the hook once he realized I was simply forgetful, not trying to sabotage my belladonna tolerance."

I returned to the basement to prepare the next batch of medicine, and during my second delivery, I arrived with questions to determine what exactly Maelin had done.

"A fight broke out during an operation."

"I heard she hit Doctor Rem."

"I heard she hit *three* guardians."

"And the patient died anyway."

"She was trying to save him."

"He was a traitor."

"I don't know all the details, Blimmery."

"If you want the full story, ask Doctor Rem."

So when my shift ended at noon, I headed straight to Doctor Rem's office on the fourth floor. It was Selection Season at the time, a six-month period when the Academy guardians were studying fifteen- and sixteen-year-olds across the Vakoi Empire to choose twenty trainees for the next cycle. With no current instructional duties on the grounds, Doctor Rem was working part-time at the Hospital, and while it was nice to have him around, I wasn't particularly cheerful about today's topic of discussion.

I peeked through the little glass window in his office door. A teenage boy seemed to be complaining about back pain, so I waited in the corridor until Doctor Rem led his patient outside and directed him to where he could pick up some medicine. That's when I asked if I could speak with him.

"Of course, Blimmery. You're always welcome here."

In his office, I took a seat on the patient's chair across from him, unable to peel my eyes from his bruise that matched Taig's.

"Wondering about this?" Doctor Rem trailed a finger along his cheek. "I'm sure you've heard the gossip, and it's true. Maelin struck me yesterday."

I shook my head, recalling the crow that she killed in the woods six years prior. Since then, I had convinced myself that she was kind, not violent. But this talk of Maelin hitting guardians was making me second-guess what little I knew about her from our minimal interactions.

"I'll tell you everything, Blimmery, but remember that we're keeping this information strictly within the Force. Guardians only. You can't go around telling City folk about our business, including your family."

"Believe it or not, Doctor, I don't tell Cousin Cove *everything* about my life."

"Good." He glanced at the door before leaning in, his voice barely above a whisper as he revealed the story.

The incident had begun at around 8:00 in the evening, when Maelin and her unit were preparing for a surgical procedure to save the life of a man who a sickly dog had attacked. If they didn't amputate his leg, the infection would spread and prove fatal.

They drugged the patient with sedatives and a controlled dose of belladonna to send him into a deep sleep, and then they got to work. Maelin cleaned his leg with alcohol as her unit members prepared tools for the procedure—scalpels for precise cuts, saws for cutting through bone, and clamps to control the bleeding.

Before making the first incision, the door burst open. Doctor Rem led Taig's Defense unit into the operating room to reveal their discovery—this patient, this *criminal*, had been collecting banned literature.

"What are you implying?" Maelin asked.

"The operation is canceled," answered Taig's unit leader. "Step away from the traitor."

The other doctors complied, but Maelin stood firm. "If we stop now, he won't wake up."

"You already drugged him," Taig said. "You put him out of his misery. It's kinder that way, remember?"

"This is different," Maelin argued, her face turning red. "We still have a chance to save him!"

"I'm sorry, Maelin," Doctor Rem said, "but you're not allowed to save him."

She ignored him, locking eyes with the commander. "How did you discover the banned literature?"

"Step away from the table," said Maelin's unit leader. "That's an irrelevant question."

"It's okay, Doctor. I don't mind answering," said Taig's unit leader. "You should remember from your studies at the Academy that Vakoi City Hospital only treats the Royal Family, the Force, and loyal City folk. With a staff of Medical guardians, it provides the best care in our Empire, and that's something we can't hand out to criminals."

Maelin tapped her boot against the floor, losing patience. A man's life was fading right in front of her, and the commander was speaking slowly, as if they were seated for lunch.

"That's why Protocol requires background checks on patients who seek treatment at our Hospital for the first time," he continued. "While your unit prepared for this emergency operation, we searched his home and discovered a hiding spot containing dozens of banned books."

"So if you find something unsavory in their possession, you sit around and watch them die?" Maelin asked.

"We deny the criminal rights to treatment and proceed with standard legal action for the crime, which would mean detainment, questioning, and potential punishment."

"So you sit around and watch them die," she concluded.

"Yes, if you must phrase it like that."

Taig took a step forward, his voice trembling. "It's just Protocol, Mae."

Maelin's eyes hopped between the commanders and doctors. There were seven other guardians in the room, and she couldn't hold them all off, but she stole a scalpel from her unit member anyway.

The guardians went quiet as Maelin made the first incision. It was impossible. How could she break Protocol right in front of them?

But once reality sunk in, her unit leader ordered her to stand down. She ignored him, leaving the commanders and doctors no choice but to physically intervene.

Taig was the only one to stand back. "Stop this!"

Maelin didn't listen.

Taig moved on, shouting at the commanders to let her go instead.

They didn't listen either.

Maelin fended off the guardians with everything she had, but it was only a matter of time before they ripped the scalpel from her hands and pushed her against the wall. The guardians surrounded her, blocking the patient from her field of vision. She tried to squeeze her way between them, and when that didn't work, she reached for the dagger in her overcoat.

Doctor Rem snatched Maelin's wrist just in time. She retaliated with a punch to his cheek, forcing Taig to join in. He tried to pry the guardians off of her, but a fist struck his face next, and he stumbled backward into the operating table. A wheeled cart of surgical tools toppled over, scattering knives around his boots that Maelin darted for, but couldn't reach in time.

"Mae!" Taig screamed so loudly that doctors could hear him from the basement floor.

CHAPTER 6

TRAITORS

Without foreseeing the consequences, the boy shattered a wall
that he once deemed impossible to walk through.

♬ BLACK CLOUD · PLAYWRITE ♬

After hearing the story from Doctor Rem, I returned to the Complex and
knocked on the door to Maelin's flat. Once again, no answer. *Are they really
keeping her at the Facility for* this *long?*

With a deep breath, I approached Kanter's flat instead. We had exchanged
no more than a few words since graduation, so I couldn't help but feel
awkward as I knocked on his door.

Kanter opened it almost instantly. "Blimmery," he acknowledged, his
expression unreadable.

"Hi. I'm wondering if you could... maybe do me a favor?"

Kanter stared, awaiting further details.

"You heard about Maelin's operation, right?"

"Everyone's heard by now."

"Is the patient's documentation available yet?"

"A full report has already been filed in the archives."

"Could you let me see it?"

His eyes narrowed slightly. "Were you assigned to write his eulogy?"

I realized I had made a mistake, asking Kanter to see files I had no right to see. I was not a professor like him with unrestricted access to the archives. And I certainly hadn't been assigned to write a eulogy for the dead traitor's funeral.

"No..." I said slowly, buying time to conjure an excuse.

"It was a joke," Kanter said with that same straight face. "I'll take you to the archives."

I chuckled. It seemed Ogga's sense of humor had rubbed off on Kanter, though his delivery lacked the same finesse.

We rode our horses to the Investigation Office, which I hadn't been to since my time as a shadow. I would have been excited, but Kanter's wild style of horseback riding gave me only *living* to focus on as I followed him. He weaved between guardian vaults and City folk like he was racing the clock, and my heart was pounding by the time we secured our horses in the stable.

Thankfully, entering the Office common room settled my nerves. Although I didn't mind working in the Hospital's serum and remediation department, I couldn't deny that I preferred the environment of professors. I loved the warmth of the Office's bookshelves, comfortable sofas, and lantern lights. *It's nice to be back.*

The few professors reading in the common room didn't seem to mind me—or the Medical badges on my shoulders—as Kanter and I headed to the archives on the second floor. He made a beeline to a file cabinet, ran his fingers along a few folders, and raised one labeled with the patient's name.

"Is that the one?" I asked.

Kanter looked at me with a tinge of disappointment. *Why do you think I grabbed it?* his eyes said. How ironic that I once thought he wasn't too bright when I now felt like an idiot around him.

We broke the file's papers into two piles, and every so often, Kanter would nod at a page he'd read and add it to my stack, which I figured was his way of saying, *Check this out, Blimmery. It's interesting stuff.*

My eyes widened when I reached a page detailing the patient's income.

"This guy was rich. Incredibly so, even for City standards. And look here —he sponsored Pandora's Box. You know, the artistic collective? My cousin's a huge fan of their plays."

Kanter's eyes hopped over the paper because he'd lost his place, and with a resigning sigh, he looked up at me. "How about we read our respective pages first, and share notes at the end?" That was his polite way of saying, *Don't interrupt me, asshole.*

As we read, I started to piece together a portrait of the deceased—his affluent lifestyle, his dysfunctional family, his patronage of the arts... I started to imagine him less like the patient involved in Maelin's operation and more like a real person.

This man had died tragically, thinking he was going into an operation he would wake from. The Force would argue that he didn't deserve to, but I wasn't sure I agreed anymore. He had a collection of banned literature, but what was so dangerous about the books that he deserved the death penalty just for possession?

He had a family. He had a career. He had an artistic collective he admired enough to sponsor. He had a whole life, and Maelin saw that before any of us did, and she was trying to honor that.

I never should have second-guessed her kindness. She only fought the guardians because she respected her patient's life, as I'm sure anyone would after reading his file.

Maelin had done the right thing, despite breaking Protocol, and this realization threatened my belief that the Force could do no wrong.

I flipped to the final page of my stack, which included the list of banned literature the guardians had found in the patient's hiding spot. Among them was the book my uncle had written, the one that destroyed my parents' careers before I revived them. *The Force's Hidden Agenda* by Meridian Owding. I had never known the title before. Everyone referred to it as the Meridian book.

For the first time, I felt a pull toward its content. The title was treasonous, as expected, but the topic took me by surprise. Uncle Meridian had written about the Force, the very organization I had vowed forty years of service to. I was a guardian now, and part of me wanted to know what my uncle would have thought of that.

"No need to share notes, Kanter. I found what I needed." I smiled at him. "Thanks for the help."

"Why wouldn't I help you? We graduated together."

I stood and peered down at him. "Would you help Taig?"

"No."

His response was so prompt that I couldn't help but laugh.

Kanter tilted his head, a frown creasing his brow.

I settled my humor and said, "I'll show myself out."

Leaving the Investigation Office went just as smoothly as entering. I slipped outside and headed for the stable, but a young girl in a Vakoi City Primary uniform stopped me by holding out a flier.

"Pandora's Box!" she said in a salesy voice. "Their best production yet! Show's in three hours at Pandora's Hall!" Then she scurried off, handing a poster to a woman passing by. "Pandora's Box at Pandora's Hall! Their best production..."

The City seemed to fall quiet as I neared the stable, reading the promotional flier. I thought of Maelin's patient, and how he had sponsored performances like this. I had never bothered to see any Pandora's Box productions growing up, despite their popularity, but right now, I couldn't contain my curiosity.

Why would Maelin's patient invest a substantial chunk of his fortune in this *artistic collective, and this one alone?* Perhaps Pandora's Box had something to say.

I'm so sorry, Maelin.

I shouldn't have gone to that play.

Pandora's Hall was an art piece in itself, flaunting walls with murals, velvety seats, and ruby curtains concealing a grand stage. I ignored the stares of City folk eyeing my uniform as I scanned the crowd for an open seat, my eyes widening at the sight of Cove. Her seaweed-green button-up shimmered obnoxiously, catching light with every move.

I squeezed past viewers in the aisle and sat beside her, scrunching my nose at the cloying lavender scent. *No wonder the seats beside her are empty.*

"Boo," I said.

Cove's jaw dropped. "Cousin Blimmery!" She wrapped me in a suffocating hug. "Oh, what a surprise!"

"Ease up on that perfume, will you?"

"Never. If I die first, you *must* promise to empty ten bottles onto my rotting corpse." She noticed the curtains unveiling and shook my shoulder with a surprisingly strong grip. "Cousin, it's starting!"

"You're not gonna ask me why I showed, after all those times you failed to drag me into this hall?"

"Shh! Explain the miracle later!"

It was an odd play about a man named Pandora who was trying to buy his way to fame. But the more items he purchased, the more people viewed him as superficial. A rather basic story with the message being, *You can't control whether or not people like you.* And to top it off, its toxic romantic subplot left us biting our nails and cringing. *I would expect Pandora's Box to write something more sophisticated than this.*

I leaned over Cove's shoulder and whispered, "Why is he named Pandora? A bit cheesy, right?"

"The main character is always Pandora," she whispered back.

"Same character in a series?"

"No, different stories. But they keep the name going to honor the lead actor."

"That's odd."

"It's an inside joke, the Pandora thing. You wouldn't get it. You're not a Panda."

"Panda?"

"It's what fans call themselves."

"Oh, you have got to be kidding—"

Someone shushed us from the aisle behind, and Cove stifled her laughter. It was just a moment later when the same man noticed my uniform in the dim light and muttered, "I apologize for being rude, Doctor. Thank you for your service."

Cove punched the Medical badge on my shoulder. "Look at you. All respected now."

I rolled my eyes, as I'm sure the man behind us did too.

"Three thousand gold coins for this one right here!" Pandora said from the stage, lugging bag after bag of clinking coins into a chest. In exchange, a woman handed him a rustic red book, which he held over his head. "Now I have acquired the book of truth! It contains all the knowledge in the world, and there will be no stopping me now! With every truth in my heart, everyone will love me, and they won't even know why! They'll simply love me because I am what they know!"

As the curtains closed, a few viewers in the crowd shuffled in their seats, murmuring to each other. I couldn't shake the feeling that I was being watched.

I flinched when the curtains reopened, revealing every actor on stage, Pandora front and center. They leaned into a synchronized bow, and the crowd roared.

I stood and offered a few lazy claps.

"Good evening, Pandas! I'm Pandora, head of the collective!" The lead actor raised the red book over his head again. "I hope to see you in two days for the annual Pandora's Box auction at Pandora's Ball, held here in Pandora's Hall! Get ready for pandemonium!"

"Masquerade ball and an auction..." I said to myself. *What an odd combination of events.* But the anonymity provided by masks, coupled with the distraction of an auction, created the ideal conditions for discreet exchanges. Perhaps the perfect conditions to sell banned books at three thousand gold coins apiece.

The crowd cheered once more, and I was sure of it then. This artistic collective was hosting more than performances, galleries, social events, and auctions. There was something suspicious going on here, and it had to do with Uncle Meridian, his banned book, and the patient Maelin had tried to save.

The feeling of someone watching me returned, pulling my eyes from the stage. I swerved my head around. Everyone was staring at Pandora— except for a guardian at the end of my row.

I squinted at Kanter, and he quickly looked away. I realized that earlier, when we had been in the archives together, I hadn't asked him what he thought about Maelin's operation incident. *Is he a fan of Pandora's Box, or is he curious about her patient too?*

As the curtains closed for the last time, Kanter slipped out of the aisle, heading for the door. I nearly went after him, hoping to catch a ride to the Complex, but Cove turned my chin to face her.

"Oh, you *must* attend the ball with me, Cousin! You *must*! Pandora's Box always puts on a show!"

I knew I needed to speak with Maelin as soon as I left Pandora's Hall. It couldn't wait.

Surely they released her from questioning by now, right?

I marched toward the Complex, regretting my choice to walk twenty minutes to the play for the sake of exercise. Kanter had ridden away like a maniac, and while I had thought of asking Cove for a ride, one of the Guardian Vows was to stay emotionally detached from the people of our lives prior to guardianship. Adherence to this Vow wasn't heavily moderated, but attracting the Force's attention was the last thing I wanted, considering what I was about to tell Maelin.

"Blimmery?" Wick spotted me from horseback as he trotted down the road. "Why are you in such a hurry?"

I stopped as he pulled up next to me. "It's a long story. Did you just leave the Facility?"

"Yeah, on my way to grab some food. I'll give you a ride if you keep me company." He patted his horse's butt.

"Maelin was being held there for questioning, right?"

"In my horse's butt?"

"Wick!"

"Calm down, Blimmery. I'm all up to speed. They released her a few hours ago, and she's still a bit riled up, but this whole thing will blow over."

I sighed. "Thank the stars... Where is she right now? With Taig, somewhere?"

Wick shook his head. "He's on an expedition, dealing with some criminals in Nominner. His unit leader wouldn't let him stay behind, and oh, how he tried. You should have been there." He cleared his throat and deepened his voice in impersonation. *"Commander, please don't make me leave the City! I have to be here for Maelin when she's released! She has no one else!"*

I chuckled. "She has no one else?"

"He thinks he's everything to her. It's hilarious." Wick grabbed the reins again. "My ass hurts from sitting here, Blimmery. If you're not joining me for supper, let me leave."

"You're dismissed."

I watched Wick ride his horse around a corner before I continued to the Complex on foot.

Twenty minutes later, I nearly knocked on Maelin's door, but then I realized I was planning to babble about Pandora's Box after she had spent an entire night being interrogated. She was likely sleep-deprived and frustrated, yet here I was, making this about me.

Dammit, Blimmery. You can never read the room.

I brewed some tea in my flat, stealing Maelin's recipe—willow bark, chamomile, and mint. The gesture felt manipulative when my real motive wasn't to cheer her up, but to tell her that I was on her side. I hoped the latter would lead to the former.

Finally, mug in hand, I knocked on her door.

When Maelin greeted me, her red eyes widened. She turned away to fix her hair, and I realized that she had probably expected Taig, not me. *I should have announced my name first.* But it was too late now, so I held out the tea.

"Thanks." She took the mug and stepped aside, inviting me in.

"Oh, I don't want to intrude."

"You made me tea, Blimmery. You intruded already. I know you wanna talk."

I took a deep breath and nodded, stepping into her flat. It looked exactly like mine. Exactly like Wick's. It was almost creepy, to walk into someone else's space and realize they were living a parallel experience to yours, with nothing but a slightly different angled view of the City from their window.

She leaned against the wall and took a sip, her face lightening a little. "You remembered the recipe, but the ratios are wrong. Too much chamomile."

"According to my father, I have a tendency to almost impress, but ultimately disappoint."

She smiled weakly. "I'm guessing you want the story?"

"Doctor Rem told me the story."

"So what do you want then?"

"To see if you're okay? Would you buy that?"

"No." She took another sip.

Maelin can handle it, I assured myself. Despite her exhaustion, she clearly wanted to hear what I wanted to tell her, so I cut to the chase.

"It's been a long day, I've given it plenty of thought, and I've come to the conclusion that—that you did the right thing."

Maelin gripped the mug tighter. "You mean it?"

"I do. Your patient didn't deserve to die. They were *just books*."

Her tone sharpened. "Are you playing a game with me, Blimmery?"

"What?"

"No one's on my side in situations like this. Not even Taig."

"I *am* on your side."

"You weren't when the guardians forced him to get his mark first. I told you how I felt that night, and you were just quiet."

"Because I didn't know how to feel back then." I broke eye contact. "And I probably wouldn't know how to feel now, either, had I not discovered something strange by accident."

She set the mug on her countertop and exhaled. "Tell me."

"I convinced Kanter to let me into the archives to read your patient's file. I was just curious about him, but then I discovered that one of the banned books he possessed was my uncle's, and it was about the Force's *hidden agenda*, and then I got *really* curious. I ended up attending a performance that Pandora's Box was putting on today, because your patient was a major sponsor. He gave the collective tons and tons of money. You wouldn't believe it."

I paused to gather my thoughts. I didn't know how to piece everything together into a single point, but I knew I had *something*.

"The play was cryptic and odd, and the main character paid exactly three thousand coins for everything he purchased, the last item being a book of truth. And then, once the show was over, they promoted an auction at their masquerade ball, which takes place the day after tomorrow."

"Pandora's Ball," Maelin deduced.

"I don't know. Maybe I'm reading too much into this, and there's nothing going on, but part of me feels like your patient purchased the banned books from Pandora's Box, and that they're having another secret book sale at the ball."

Maelin took a minute to process my story.

"I don't think you're reading into it too much," she decided. "I think you're reading into it just right. I've had a feeling, ever since the branding ceremony, that the Force isn't good. I wouldn't be surprised if others feel this way too. People like your uncle. Maybe the Force didn't execute him because his work was endangering people. Maybe they executed him because his work was endangering *them*."

I took a step toward her. "If I say this, do you promise you won't tell Taig?"

"There's a lot of things I don't tell Taig."

"I know it's crazy, but part of me wants to buy the Meridian book, and —and read it. To find out what it is my Uncle wrote about the Force that made them kill him."

Maelin stared at me, dead in the eye. It looked like she had been waiting for this moment for a long time.

"Blimmery?"

"Yes?"

"Let's go to the stupid ball."

This book may be a death sentence, but my need
to write it overpowers my fear of the consequences.
Sharing the truth wide and far will slowly diminish the
burden of knowing it. Unkept secrets hold no power.
So let us speak, my friend, and let us be loud.

THE FORCE'S HIDDEN AGENDA

MERIDIAN OWDING

PART 2

KNOWLEDGE

CHAPTER 7

GRAVEDIGGER

With each repetition, a lie, however well-intentioned,
further blinds its teller to the truth.

♫ HEARING DAMAGE - THOM YORKE ♫

Later that night, as I lay in bed, a series of faint knocks echoed from the hallway. I ignored them at first, pushing my pillows to my ears and focusing on my nightly battle of drifting off. But the noise didn't stop.

With a sigh, I slipped out of bed, cracked my door open, and peeked into the hallway. Taig stood at Maelin's door, still in uniform with his dual swords strapped to his back. *His expedition must have run late.*

Taig knocked again. "Mae," he called, his voice barely reaching my ears.

I stepped into the hallway. "There's no point in whispering if you plan to wake the whole floor with your knocking anyway."

Taig paused, eyes locked on Maelin's door. "You're the only one with sleep problems, Blim Blim. So instead of whining, why don't you suck your thumb, self-soothe, and crawl back into bed?"

"You should have gone into childcare."

Taig scoffed, finally facing me, and his watery eyes broke my humor.

He hasn't spoken with Maelin since yesterday's operation, has he? It was the longest I'd seen them apart.

"She *is* here, right?" Taig asked, his voice softer.

"She's probably knocked out. Exhausted."

"But do you know if she's... fine?"

I nodded. "She said she has a week off service to attend correctional meetings—just a few hours a day to talk about what happened. If all goes well, she'll go right back to her usual schedule."

"That's good," Taig said, more to himself than to me. "Yeah, maybe she *should* talk about it more. Get it out of her system."

"Get *what* out of her system?" I asked, my tone harsher than expected. *Why is everyone acting like she lost her mind when all she did was try to save a life?*

"You weren't there, Blim. She was..."

"She was what?"

Taig shook his head, refusing to finish, and headed for his flat down the hall.

I was reentering mine when he finally muttered, "Thanks."

It was the first time he had ever expressed gratitude for me, but I pretended not to hear him and shut my door.

The next morning, I worked on pure habit, trusting my muscle memory not to make any mistakes. I could handle another scolding from my unit leader. What I *couldn't* handle was suffering the consequences of getting caught purchasing the Meridian book.

At noon, when my half-day Hospital shift ended, I headed straight to the road behind Pandora's Hall, our established meeting point. Maelin was already there, standing by her white horse and petting its mane.

How long ago did her first correctional meeting end? What was it like? How does she feel now? A string of questions threatened to find their way to my tongue, but I resisted for the time being.

"You ready?" I asked, pulling my horse up next to hers.

"I've been ready forever." She gave her horse a final pat before mounting it. "How far?"

"Twenty minutes," I said, trotting forward to lead the way.

We rode our horses to Cove's place, a modest one-story cabin located on the outskirts of Vakoi City, surrounded by trees that blocked most of the daylight. It felt like evening when we arrived, as the neon lanterns lining the roof overhang, swaying gently in the wind, did little to combat the darkness.

"I never imagined your cousin living in the woods," Maelin said as we secured our horses in Cove's stable.

"I never imagined myself living in the Complex."

"People aren't always what they seem. Is that what you're saying?"

I laughed. "I'm not being philosophical. I'm just saying what I'm saying."

As we made our way toward the front steps, my smile faded at the sight of Cove's handmade flag—which featured the Academy's four-petaled flower emblem—flapping from a pole by the cabin. I wished I didn't have to fool her into helping Maelin and me break a Guardian Vow, but if she knew the truth, she wouldn't help us willingly.

We scaled the steps, ducking under the hanging lanterns. One of them swung into Maelin's head, and she chuckled. "Why are they so low?"

"My cousin likes being an inconvenience." I knocked on the front door, and in a hushed tone, counted down from ten. Right as I hit *one*, Cove yelled, "Just a minute!" through the wall.

"She orchestrated that?" Maelin asked.

"She's a master manipulator. Went to acting intensives every summer before she realized she wanted to design *for* artistic collectives, not perform in them."

The door swung open, revealing Cove with a spool of thread in her hand and a strip of fabric draped over her shoulder, as though she was in the middle of working. She cast the props away at the sight of us.

"Cousin Blimmery!" Cove exclaimed, ruffling my hair. "And it's Doctor Maelin, right?"

"Just Maelin is fine."

"You have my *massive* respect for surviving eighteen months at the Academy with this one."

I swatted Cove's hand away and smoothed my hair back into place, my cheeks warming as Maelin laughed. *It's not like we were around each other much,* I wanted to argue. *Taig made sure of that.*

"Well, hurry in! But take those grimy boots off first. I'd hate to discover what atrocities are lying around on the Hospital floors."

After removing our boots, Maelin and I stepped into the living room with our matching black socks, and my shoulders dropped instantly. Cove's cabin was oddly comforting—a disorganized mess, but not *my* kind of disorganized. I was the type to leave clothes lying about and forget to close drawers, but Cove's kind of mess was the intentional kind. Framed design plans decorated the walls in crooked angles that mirrored each other on opposite sides of the room, and colorful lanterns hung in the order of the rainbow.

Cove sat at her desk, placed awkwardly in the middle of the living room. "What can I do for you?" She gestured to the client chairs across from her.

I took a seat. "If I recall correctly, you owe me a favor."

Cove rolled her eyes. "That was one time."

"Two times." I held my fingers up. "Two."

Maelin lingered on foot for a few more seconds, scanning the living room, before sitting beside me and smiling at Cove. "What'd you make him do?"

"Oh, you know..." Cove looked away, puckering her lips. "I might have asked my cousin to pull his guardian card to get me into a couple of invite-only parties."

"Yes," I said, "and to return the massive favors, I'd like you to lend us your work for Pandora's Ball."

Cove's face lit up. "You're attending?"

"Unfortunately."

"Oh, I can't believe it! You will *not* regret this, Cousin!" She sprung to her feet and leaned toward me, palms on her desk. "Yes, of course I'll help you! But you *must* know that I'm doing it out of the goodness of my heart, not because I owe you. We broke even after you seated me next to your brother for supper last week."

"He's sixteen. Not a little brat anymore."

"A grown brat is still a brat." Cove shuffled through a cluttered drawer. "Now shut your mouth so I can focus on designing the most amazing masks you've ever seen. They'll suit your formal wear flawlessly." She slammed a notebook onto her desk, armed herself with a pen, and peered down at Maelin. "Remind me of the color of your dress? I can't recall if it was more of a peach or a salmon."

Maelin's brows knitted together. "I—uh—well, Blimmery and I weren't —we weren't thinking of—"

Her nervousness was starting to make *me* nervous, so I took over. "We're actually planning to wear something else to the ball."

Cove squinted at me. "Something else?"

I wiped my clammy palms on my pants. Cove knew that guardians vowed to wear only their sanctioned uniforms and formal wear in public, unless granted undercover clearance.

"It's for an undercover task. That's all I can say."

Cove stared for a moment longer before breaking a grin and placing a hand on her heart. "Aww, you're going undercover, and you could have gone to any designer in the City, but you came here? You must love me to pieces." Her feathery dress waved behind her as she rushed across the room to a rack of rentals. "Let's see your talented cousin at work. Come over here, you two, and help me choose..."

The guilt started to pile in my chest as Maelin and I picked potential outfits for the ball, but I knew this was the only way. If we were to wear our uniforms, Pandora's Box would never sell us a treasonous book— guardians were known for *killing* people who possessed them. On the other hand, if we were to show up in our formal wear, there was a chance they'd recognize us from Imperial ceremonies they had also attended.

It's no big deal, I thought to myself. *Cousin Cove won't find out.* No one *will find out.*

After we made our final choices, Cove insisted on altering them to perfection. She took Maelin's measurements first, and when she moved on to me, Maelin sauntered around the living room, studying the framed sketches.

Cove wrapped her measuring tape around my chest and leaned in. "Is something bad happening at the ball?" she whispered.

I shook my head far too many times. The last thing I wanted was to burden Cove with paranoia after I'd already lied to her face.

"Well, whatever you're doing, please be careful, Cousin."

"I will," I muttered, and with a gentle hand on my shoulder, she unraveled the measuring tape.

"Maelin?" Cove called, stealing her eyes from a framed design. "Do you have time to stay for lunch?"

Maelin glanced at me and smiled. "I'd love to stay."

"Oh, of course you would! That's why I asked if you had time, silly." Cove checked the clock. "Stick around for another hour. I want to get these alterations done first."

"I'm afraid you don't know what you've signed up for, Maelin," I said. "My cousin is a terrible cook. I once found a needle in my sandwich."

"Hey!" Cove threw a spool of thread at my back, making me jump. "You swore never to speak of that!"

"You nearly gave me a piercing," I added, and Maelin laughed.

Cove waved her finger at me. "You watch your tongue, Cousin."

"Oh, you bet I'll be watching my tongue, considering your needle-nightmare of a sandwich." I chucked the spool of thread back at her, and she caught it with a grin.

As Cove altered our pieces, I showed Maelin the backyard, where a small courtyard led to the beach. We could smell the salty breeze from the City center, where the Complex and Hospital were located, but we lived too far away to hear and see the waves crashing into the sand like this.

Maelin took her socks off and crossed the courtyard.

"I'm sorry if my cousin's a lot to handle," I called after her.

"Don't worry, Blimmery. I'm not staying for lunch out of obligation." She faced me and backstepped toward the ocean, her feet in the sand. "Are you coming?"

With my socks still on, I jogged to catch up to her, leaving the tree shade behind and entering the sunlight. We came to a halt where the dry met damp and stared out at the horizon together, our palms raised to shield our eyes. The sun felt too strong after we'd spent close to half an hour in the dim light of Cove's cabin.

"Hey, Maelin?"

"I don't want to talk about the meeting, Blimmery. I just want to stand here."

I nodded. "Okay."

It could have been a few seconds that we stood there, or a few minutes. I can't be sure. But I remember feeling, for a moment, like I was free from expectations. Our hunt for the Meridian book was the first task I'd chosen for myself in years. I wasn't doing this because the Force told me to, or my family expected me to. I was doing this for me.

I wonder if anyone feels like this all the time.

The waves lulled me into a different world, so deeply that I was surprised to hear Maelin's voice again.

"Your cousin has a beautiful home."

She looked less tired now, as though standing here in the sand had rejuvenated her too, and she was no longer burdened with what she had done in the operating room and how it made other guardians feel.

Finally, I processed her statement. "She has another home in the City center too. It's much classier, but she's hardly there."

"That's not her home, then."

"Well, she owns it."

"That's not what I mean. People only have one home."

I looked away with a grin. I understood what Maelin meant, and it was too serious for my liking. "Are we going to debate the existence of souls and reincarnation too?"

"You're insanely lucky to have her," she replied, ignoring my remark. "Are you as close to your immediate family?"

"Absolutely not. My relationships with my parents and brother are a bit... rocky."

"And yet you suffered the program for them."

I shrugged. "They're family. I can't stand them, but for some reason, I can't stand hating them either."

"If that's your definition of family, Taig and I check the box."

A voice in my head warned me not to pry, but I suppressed it. "What do you mean?"

"There are parts of me that Taig can't stand. And I can't stand that he tries to change those parts of me."

I thought back to that day in Brackle Beans when Maelin had implied that her work as a Medical guardian wasn't the most important thing she could be doing. She had a tendency to diminish the Force's image, and Taig hated that, but I was starting to admire her reckless side. Unlike me, she didn't allow expectations to sway her every action.

"Cove said you had supper at your parents' place last week," Maelin added, changing the subject. "Do you get visitation rights often?"

I hesitated, suddenly aware of my casual disregard for Protocol. Most guardians had grown up more than an hour away and needed official permission for family visits, but my family lived here, in the same place I worked in. I'd taken for granted the ease of bending the rules for my convenience, seeing them as I pleased.

"It's okay," Maelin replied to my silence. "It's not like I'd report you, and if I did, I doubt the Force would care. A crime like yours is nothing compared to a crime like mine."

My gaze found the horizon again. "What you did wasn't a crime."

"It's a crime in *The Guardian Handbook*."

I smirked. "That's not what I mean."

She chuckled and faced the ocean with me. "Your parents' place—is it home to you?"

"Not anymore."

"How about the Complex?"

"Yes," I said, then shook my head. "Well, no. Not really."

"The Academy?"

"*Nightmare* Academy?"

"Where is your home, then?"

I looked back at Cove's cabin without a second thought, frowning as I realized what I'd done. It felt silly, but I said, "Here."

Maelin smiled.

"How about you?" I asked.

"Here," she echoed, her eyes locked on a crashing wave.

After enjoying a lunch of overly sweet soup, Maelin and I stopped at a bank to withdraw three thousand coins. We split the velvet pouches between our book bags, which could barely close to conceal our money. The weight made us walk at a slight angle, and by the time we scaled the front steps to the Complex, our shoulders were sore. We clutched our bag straps to lighten the pressure.

"I can't imagine hauling this around the ball," Maelin said. "Why don't we pay with a bill of exchange? I bet that's how the other so-called *sponsors* pay for their books."

"Except our bills of exchange have our names on them, with the honorific *Doctor*," I argued. "Not to mention the Academy emblem, and the Imperial stamp."

"I guess you're right. But you don't have to be all sassy about it." Maelin swung the front door open, her grin fading at the sight of Taig.

"Mae!" He stopped pacing the common room and rushed toward her. "Where the hell have you been?"

She glanced at me as we walked inside. "We were... out for a bit."

"Together?"

Maelin pursed her lips when Taig stopped in front of her, crossing his arms. Her darting eyes and fidgeting hands reminded me of how nervous she had looked when Cove asked about the color of her dress. *Perhaps Maelin's a terrible liar because she so often speaks her mind, and Taig knows that.*

Giving up on a response, he turned to me.

"We ran into each other on the way here," I explained. "She just left her correctional meeting."

"Is that true, Mae?" Taig asked, his eyes still on me.

Maelin finally looked at him. "You know it's not true, so why ask? If you're going to antagonize me after I haven't seen you for two days, then I'd rather not talk to you at all!"

Before he could reply, Maelin stormed past him.

"Bitterview being bitter," I said. "What's new?"

"Mae." Taig took a step toward her. "Mae, come on…"

"Don't follow me," she snapped, disappearing up the staircase.

Taig took a deep breath before frowning at me. "Wick said her meeting was over this morning, and I know you work half-days at the Hospital. I've been waiting around for two hours now, so the least you could do is give me a straight answer."

I searched my brain for a new lie more believable than the last. It had to be something that would piss him off, but not *too* much. It couldn't be treasonous, romantic, or anything that would end with my organs scattered across the Complex common room.

"Fine…" I faked a sigh. "I brought her to the archives. Kanter let us in."

"What for?"

"To read her patient's file."

Taig scoffed, taking a few steps away as though my words were so overwhelming he couldn't even look at me. I rolled my eyes when he rubbed his temple. *How dramatic.*

"She was curious about him," I continued. "I-I thought she might find closure."

"No." Taig marched back up to me. "Closure isn't real, Blim Blim. It's a made-up concept people create because they'd rather cling to their pasts than go through the pain of healing."

"Wow, that was truly insightful. Can you say it again so I can write it down?" I reached for the notebook in my overcoat, but he pushed my hand away.

"Listen." Taig towered over me, lowering his voice. "Mae's being sent to correction right now. The guardians are keeping a close eye on her. If you care about her *at all*, you won't encourage this kind of behavior. They need to see that she's moving on from what happened, not backing further into it."

He was right, as always. The Force wouldn't forgive what Maelin and I were doing. Our plan was putting us both in danger—Maelin more than me—but we were being careful. No one at Pandora's Ball would recognize us.

The guardians would never find out.

I swallowed my pride and forced my smile away, pretending to succumb to his intimidation.

"I'm sorry," I muttered. "I thought I was helping."

"Well, you better *stop* helping, because if you pull something like this again, I'll kill you, Blim. I will." Taig spoke in an exaggerated manner, as though he was making an empty threat just for the sake of scaring me, but I gulped anyway. *I bet a small, vicious part of him isn't exaggerating in the least.*

"Because I just *know* that if I don't interfere, you'll dig her a grave, and she'll dive right into it."

CHAPTER 8

IMPOSTER

Is freedom truly freedom if it's achieved by breaking the law,
or does it mirror the thrill of a child staying up past bedtime?

♫ UNKIND · TAYLOR BRADSHAW ♫

Two days after being filled with chairs for the play, Pandora's Hall was now an open space with serving tables and golden platters along the walls. Members of the collective, dressed in black suits and golden bow ties, made rounds delivering alcoholic beverages to masked attendees.

Cove had altered a shiny black suit with a blood-red button-up for me that would be perfect for Taig's funeral, if the lucky day were to ever arrive. I had also slicked my hair back in a style I despised and swapped my midnight boots with red ones that matched my button-up, paired with tacky silver laces. The outfit made me look like an uptight, devilish clown.

But despite my perfect disguise, I couldn't shake my paranoia. The punishments for breaking Vows weren't clearly outlined in *The Guardian Handbook* like they were for Protocol violations. *If we're recognized tonight, how will the Force react?*

One of the servers made brief eye contact with me, and in that fleeting moment, I was fully convinced he recognized me.

Did I meet him at an Imperial ceremony? I adjusted my silver mask which clung to the top half of my face, making my cheeks sweat. *Maybe I crossed paths with him on the street in my uniform, or brought him medicine in the Hospital when he was a patient, or—*

"Stop looking stressed," Maelin said. "We blend right in."

I lost sight of the server and sighed. "How do you know?"

Maelin gave me a look that said, *Seriously?* and gestured to her frilly dress. It wasn't a soft yellow, but a striking shade, with black lace lining the hems and a navy-blue ribbon cinching her waist. Cove had pinned Maelin's hair into a braided bun and had applied some makeup, including black lipstick and gray eyeshadow, visible through the holes in her yellow mask. Had I not known she was Maelin, I wouldn't have recognized her.

"You're right," I said, nodding. "We're invisible."

Maelin and I had taken every possible precaution. We even carried our three thousand coins in book bags we had purchased earlier that day, just in case a fellow guardian familiar with our usual ones would be attending the ball. Our plan had no cracks.

"Let's walk." Maelin turned slowly, wobbly on her blue heels. "It's weird if we just stand here."

I cringed and caught up to her. "Try not to waddle."

"You think I had opportunities to dress up at the orphanage?"

"Why didn't you wear flats tonight?"

"Because Maelin wears flats, and tonight, I'm not her."

We halted when the ruby curtains unveiled, revealing a five-person band on stage.

"What a night, Pandas!" greeted the lead vocalist. "Am I right?" She strummed a guitar chord, and attendees whirled into the middle of the room, dancing as the air filled with song.

Maelin leaned toward me, speaking in a hushed tone. "What exactly are we looking for?"

A server swept by, slipping wine glasses into our hands.

"Something off." I took a sip.

"That's helpful."

"Like I said, it was a cryptic play."

"Hmm..." Maelin sipped her wine and cringed. "*Ugh.* I hate this stuff."
She handed the glass to another server passing by and said, "Away with it!"

I laughed. "You fit right in."

"Focus, Blimmery," Maelin snapped.

"Right." I scanned the room with a smile, feeling more at ease. "There
has to be another gathering..."

Pandora's Hall featured countless doors on every wall, most of which
appeared to be locked, as streamers and lanterns hung from the ceiling to
block them.

"There's only two doors that aren't covered," Maelin whispered. "The
one leading to the restrooms, and that one there." She pointed to the second
door, and I squinted, the poster on the wall next to it catching my eye. It
featured an illustration of Pandora holding the red book of truth over his
head. *Why would they keep the promotional poster up when the event already
passed?*

"Let me see if it's open." I parted from Maelin, gripping the strap of my
book bag to lighten its weight as I weaved through the crowd. My eyes
found Cove in the mix, wearing an icy blue dress and a matching mask with
frost-like glitter. She smirked as I passed, as though to say, *Your undercover
secret is safe with me, Cousin.*

I smiled back before I lost sight of her, the guilt piling a little higher in
my chest.

When I reached the door, I handed my glass to a server passing by, peered
over my shoulder, and discreetly twisted the doorknob. It wouldn't budge.

Please, show me a sign, I thought, facing the poster. Apart from the play's
title and its surpassed showing date, there was no text. Even the book of
truth's cover was blank, untitled. I stopped studying the illustrated props
behind Pandora when a shadow cast over me, sending a chill down my
spine.

"What do you think the book represents?" asked a man with a deep,
husky voice.

Despite the stranger's mysterious appearance, I couldn't be certain of
his connection to the secret sale, so I crafted my reply with caution.

"Pandora called it the book of truth," I said, staring at the poster. "I assume it's something not commonly read."

The man leaned over my shoulder and whispered, "Something dangerous?"

My heart skipped a beat as I faced the brawny man in a corduroy suit. A blood-orange cat mask concealed his face—with the exception of his stubbly chin and glistening smile. In his outstretched hand was a business card.

"First-timer?"

With a nod, I took the card and dropped my head to read it.

Over, under, around, and through.

By the time I looked back up, the stranger had already vanished into the crowd.

Of course Pandora's Box would turn directions into a riddle. I tucked the card into my breast pocket and searched for something related to the hint. It took about a minute to notice that the door leading to the restrooms had a sign labeled *Restrooms over here* above it.

I grinned. *There you are!*

Maelin was mid-discussion with a woman in a fur-lined suit and a fox mask when I waved at her. She nodded subtly, hinting that she'd attempt an exit once a natural pause allowed.

In the meantime, I walked along the outskirts of the hall and pretended to survey the golden platters of food. *I was right from the start. I can't believe it.* My smile widened as I quickened my pace. *We're actually going to purchase the Meridian book!*

My book bag struck a man's hip, and the clinking of coins against the marble floor shattered my smile. A few eyes darted my way as I dropped to my knees, sweeping the spilled coins back into the velvet pouch that had jumped free.

The man I'd run into crouched beside me to help. I nearly apologized to him, but he spoke first.

"Do you have your eye on a piece they're auctioning?"

Recognizing his voice, I looked up to find Kanter kneeling beside me, dressed in his guardian formal wear—a midnight-blue suit—and a simple mask with star sequins.

I fought the lingering urge to apologize and nodded, fearing one word would expose me as an imposter. *If I recognized his voice, he would recognize mine.*

Kanter handed me the coins he'd gathered, which I returned to the velvet pouch and tucked into my book bag. As soon as I stood, I spotted Maelin approaching me.

Go away. I widened my eyes at her, but she didn't get the message. Only when Kanter stood beside me did she freeze.

I peeked at Kanter, who raised his brows at Maelin. He studied her yellow and blue dress with an intensity that made me hold my breath. *He knows.*

"I'm confused," Kanter said, stepping toward her.

Maelin pursed her lips.

"I..." Kanter chuckled. "I didn't know someone could be so beautiful."

Despite the awful timing, I could barely withhold my laughter. I turned my face away, pressing a palm over my mouth. *What got into you since graduation, Kanter?*

He held his hand out with a smile. "May I have this dance?"

Maelin looked at me, and I nodded, fearing that if she were to shake her head and walk off, Kanter would grow suspicious—assuming he wasn't already.

When she finally took his hand, I couldn't stop a chuckle from slipping between my fingers, but thankfully, Kanter didn't seem to hear. He led Maelin away, and she sent me a scowl over her shoulder.

I dropped my palm, mouthing an exaggerated *aww.*

They danced as I watched from the sidelines, and it felt like I was reliving our graduation ball four years ago. *Stop dancing like you danced back then, Maelin.* I folded my hands together in hopes that Kanter wouldn't notice something familiar about her lips behind the makeup, or her eyes through the mask.

When the song ended, the band didn't lead into a new number, and the prolonged silence left the crowd muttering in anticipation.

With a single, piercing violin note, Pandora ran into view, joining the musicians on stage. "Welcome, Pandas!"

The crowd cheered and rushed toward him in a stampede. Amid the chaos, Maelin slipped away from Kanter.

"I'm Pandora, head of the collective!"

Another burst of cheers and screams. A teenage girl yelled, "Marry me, Pandora!"

"Welcome to Pandora's Ball, held here in Pandora's Hall!" he continued. "Pandora's Box is proud to present our greatest event of the year! Who's ready for our most extravagant Pand-auction yet?"

More cheering, followed by attendees throwing gold coins into the air. I held a hand over my face to shield them from hitting my eyes.

Another member of the collective walked on stage with a suit—the same one Pandora had worn during the play two days prior.

"Here we have the official costume from the latest Pandora's Play, donned by me, Pandora, head of the collective! What do you say, Pandas? Do I hear one hundred?"

"One hundred Panda coins!" a man yelled from the crowd.

Maelin appeared next to me. "Am I hallucinating, or did I hear that right?"

"I'm afraid you heard that right," I replied.

"They have their own currency?"

"I bet it's an inside joke." I lowered my voice. "Does Kanter know it's us?"

"I don't think so. We didn't talk."

"Good."

"Please tell me you found something."

I nodded, gesturing to the door.

We slipped into a dark, torch-lit hallway, the screams and shouts muffled through the wall behind us. To our left were the restroom doors, and past them were a long string of additional ones. I read their signs as we made our way down.

"What now?" Maelin asked.

"We're looking for the word *under*." I whipped out the business card long enough for her to read the message before tucking it back into my breast pocket.

"Nice. Fill me in later." Maelin scanned the hallway and pointed to a door on the left. "There." The sign next to it read, *Dressing room under construction.*

I opened the door and entered an actor's dressing room—under no construction of any kind. It was darker than in the hallway with only one lantern lighting the space.

Maelin closed the door behind us, and I squinted, noticing a ripped page on a wooden vanity. *First aid kit around the corner.*

"Around the corner," I whispered to Maelin, holding up the note. She met eyes with me before approaching a window *near* the corner, covered with velvety curtains that matched the stage's.

My jaw dropped when she pulled the curtains aside. Behind them was not a window, but a concealed hallway.

"Are you kidding?" Maelin asked. "What is this, a mystery novel?"

"I'd call it a thriller."

She entered first, her voice echoing through the hallway. "Of course you would..."

I joined her and drew the curtains shut behind us. The only light source in the hallway was a glow emanating from an opening in the floor toward the dead end. A ladder led through it into the basement, and above it was a final sign that read, *Through here.*

We descended into a cramped, hardly furnished basement room, joining a gathering of about a dozen attendees. They examined us before refocusing on a maskless woman who I recognized as an actor from the play. She held a book above her head and announced a title I'd never heard of.

"I'll take it," said a man in a green suit and a leafy mask.

An elderly woman beside me raised her hand. "I'll take one too." Her dress shimmered with an intense white that strained my eyes.

"We only have one copy this time," said the actor, pointing to the first claimant. "It goes to the man in green."

The woman in white rolled her eyes, and her mask of cracked mirrors reflected my look of realization. *The sale operates on a first-come, first-served basis. I need to be quick.*

Pulling a bank book and pen out of his blazer, the man in green approached the actor. I assumed he wrote a sum of three thousand coins on the payment line and labeled *Pandora's Box sponsorship* as the purpose.

With a nod, the actor took the bill and offered the book in return, which the man in green slipped into his blazer. She then surveyed a bookshelf behind her for the next banned title to offer, settling on a rustic red one. A few *oohs* and *aahs* filled the room as she held it up.

"*The Force's Hidden Agenda* by Meridian Owding."

My hand shot into the air. "I'll take it!"

The elderly woman chuckled at my eagerness.

Maelin rushed to catch up to me as I shoved myself through the group, reaching the actor before anyone could think to steal my claim. When we opened our book bags to pay, the actor burst into laughter. It didn't take long for the attendees to catch on and laugh too.

"This isn't an alleyway drug deal!" the actor exclaimed.

The laughter intensified, and my face ran hot. "We didn't know you accepted bills of exchange."

"Always the paranoid first-timers!" said the man in green.

The actor shook my shoulder, her laughter trailing off. "Oh, we're just messing with you, but next time, remember that we're not low-lifes here, okay?"

"Okay," I said, resisting the urge to scoff.

When the attendees settled down, the actor pointed to a scale by the bookshelf. Maelin and I transferred our coin pouches onto it, and after verifying the weight to amount to three thousand coins, the actor handed me the Meridian book.

"What a great first pick," she said.

I sat next to Maelin on the shaggy rug in Cove's guest bedroom, the fireplace and a few scattered lanterns illuminating my uncle's book in an ominous light.

How could something so small be so dangerous?

It was thinner than I'd imagined, thin enough that Maelin and I had decided to read it together in one sitting. With Cove still occupied at Pandora's Ball, we likely had a few hours alone to finish the book before our inevitable return to the Complex.

A breeze from the open window attempted to rustle Maelin's hair, and as if granting nature's wish, she pulled Cove's pins and ties out. Her braids untangled into waves as she tilted her head, staring at me through her yellow mask.

I quickly looked down at the book.

"Blimmery," she muttered, "I've been wondering something."

"What is it?" I asked.

"Back at the Academy, you always called your uncle a bad man."

I closed my eyes, inhaling a breath. It took a minute to gather my thoughts. "I think... I only called him bad because I didn't know him."

"You didn't?"

"Not really." I removed my silver mask, allowing the window breeze to brush my cheeks. "Uncle Meridian didn't get along with my family. He hated writing—even reading. Ended up working as an Imperial messenger, delivering articles for *Capital Weekly* across the Empire. And then, out of nowhere, he wrote this book and ruined our family name. If it weren't for him, I never would have joined the Academy, and I resented him for that. But I didn't *know* him."

"Do you still think he's bad?"

"I'll decide after I read his book." I met Maelin's gaze again. "For now, maybe you can answer something I've been wondering too."

"Ask me."

I waved my silver mask in the air. "Why would you do all of this with me? Break a Vow, piss off Taig, go to the ball? What benefit could you get out of reading my uncle's book?"

"I'm hoping to find proof that I'm not crazy."

I frowned, and set my mask down. "You're *not* crazy, Maelin. You don't need a book to prove that."

"Yes, I do. I've heard the gossip, Blimmery. We both know you're the only guardian who doesn't judge me for what I did during that operation." Maelin removed her yellow mask and tossed it aside. "If there's anyone I trust the most, it's Taig, but even *he* thinks I'm crazy. He's always trying to silence me."

"He's just worried because he loves you." I didn't know where that sentence came from, or why I was so quick to say it.

"I know," Maelin replied, "but he doesn't *know* me."

"Of course he knows you."

She shook her head. "Not this part of me."

There was something different about her gaze now, something magnetizing. For a moment, I feared I was leaning toward her, and I feared even more that she might be leaning toward me too.

She smiled, just slightly. My heart was pounding in my ears because we'd been staring into each other's eyes for too long to be normal, but looking away seemed wrong. I couldn't win.

Another window breeze rustled our hair, and in unison, we pulled free from whatever had grasped us, returning our focus to the book.

"I still can't believe we bought this." I reached for the cover, but Maelin caught my wrist with a gentle touch.

She leaned in and whispered, "Do you hear that?"

I flinched when the door burst open.

"Guess who's home?" Cove sang, waltzing into the guest bedroom. I didn't have time to hide the book, and her smile crumbled at the sight of it. "What are you doing?"

My throat tightened. "I-It's just a book we were—"

"I know what book it is."

I hopped to my feet, hugging the Meridian book to my chest. "Cousin, please, it's—"

"Don't *Cousin* me, Blimmery," she snapped, creeping forward. "You said this was for an undercover task, but this was all to... You fooled me so you could meet with some dealer at the ball, and..." She halted, her scowl morphing into a pout as she covered her face with her palms.

Maelin stood and joined my side. "I'm sorry, Cove. It was my idea."

"I hated lying to you," I said, "but I—"

"Are you *crazy*?" Cove dropped her hands, revealing her red cheeks. "You could be killed just for possession. What if someone recognized you?"

"No one did," I assured her.

"If anyone finds out, I could get pulled into it too." Cove's eyes widened. "I helped you do this."

"It's okay. You didn't know."

"As if they'd believe my ignorance!" Her shoulders rose and fell as she struggled to settle her breaths. "Did you read it?"

I shook my head.

"Give it to me." She held her hand out, and I took a step back.

"No."

"Blimmery." She closed the gap. "I need to get rid of it!"

"There's no way I'm letting you—"

"Stop!" Maelin shouted, shoving herself between Cove and me. "Both of you!"

We glared at each other over Maelin's shoulder.

"We already have the book." Maelin continued, her voice soft despite the tension in the bedroom. "What's done is done, so we might as well read it, but Cove's right too—we can't be accused of possession. So I say we finish the book quickly, then burn it. No one ever has to know."

Cove's expression lightened, and I could tell she wasn't completely opposed to the idea.

"You can read it with us," I offered, the frustration in my voice lifting. "Aren't you a *little* curious about what Uncle wrote?"

"He was a bad man. He ruined your parents' reputation."

"But what if he wrote something that was *worth* ruining my parents' reputation for?"

Cove shook her head, her eyes watering. "Oh, Cousin..."

I stepped around Maelin and offered Cove the book, proving I trusted her to follow through with our compromise.

"Please?" I asked.

Cove stared at me for a long time before reaching out and taking *The Force's Hidden Agenda* into her shaky hands. Maelin and I joined her on either side, and as she flipped to the first page, a door opened that could never be closed again.

CHAPTER 9

PROTECTOR

It's not unusual for those who know dangerous truths to cling to safe illusions, unknowingly forging the chains that bind them.

♫ AN HONEST MISTAKE - MATING RITUAL ♫

I woke to the sound of crashing waves, and the smell of pancakes—a stark contrast to the Complex's slamming doors and marching boots. I hadn't spent a night outside my flat in the four years since moving in.

Rubbing my eyes, I sat up to find myself in Cove's guest bed. I was still dressed in the stiff suit I had worn to Pandora's Ball, and it took a moment for me to recall what had happened after we read the Meridian book. *Cousin Cove went to her room in tears while Maelin tossed the book into the fireplace, and then we...*

My eyes shot to the empty space beside me, where Maelin had slept. Even though nothing happened, my face ran hot anyway. We were guardians, and we had spent the night outside the Complex together.

Hopefully no one noticed. I slipped out of bed. "Maelin?"

A torn notebook page on the nightstand caught my eye.

Gone for my correctional meeting. See you at the Complex.

I sighed. I had forgotten about her morning meetings. *How could she handle speaking to a guardian for three hours when the mere thought of seeing one makes me sick?*

The smell of pancakes and the sizzling of a pan led me to the kitchen, where Cove stood at the stove with a spatula in hand. She was dressed in a plain green shirt with gray pants, the most simple clothes I had ever seen her in.

Cove noticed my shadow on the wall and looked over her shoulder. "Hey. I was just about to wake you." I should have known not to expect a chirpy *Rise and shine, Cousin!*

I took a seat at the dining table, and a few minutes later, she set two plates down, followed by a pair of tea cups.

"You didn't have to cook me breakfast," I said.

"Who said I made you breakfast?" She sat across from me. "This is all mine."

I managed a weak grin and grabbed my fork. The food was overly sweet, as Cove always liked it. I usually minded, but during that bitter morning, I didn't. I plopped another sugar cube into my tea. *If only I could vanish and live a quiet life like this, somewhere far from the City.*

Cove set her fork down. "What now, Cousin?"

I shrugged, gazing at the rippling tea in my cup. "How am I supposed to go back to work," I whispered, "and pretend that I'm clueless?"

For the first time in my life, Cove had nothing encouraging to say. She had nothing to say at all.

About an hour later, I mustered the courage to put my uniform on and leave Cove's cabin. It was nearly noon when I approached the Complex, spotting a red-faced Taig rushing down the front steps.

My heart skipped a beat. *Does he know that Maelin and I weren't in our flats last night?* Perhaps he had knocked on our doors to discover that we both hadn't answered.

Taig reached me right as I pulled my horse up to the stable.

"Look, whatever you think happened—"

"Get out of my way, Blim!"

I frowned, realizing that he didn't know about last night after all. His eyes were not on me, but the stable doors my horse had blocked.

"What's going on?" I asked.

He turned away, shaking his head as a hollow laugh escaped him. "Just move your damn horse."

"Tell me where you're going first."

With a sharp pivot, he was facing me again, reaching for the dagger in his overcoat.

I tightened my grip on the reins, fighting the urge to trot forward and clear his path. I couldn't let him leave. If something had made him *this* upset, surely it had to do with Maelin. The Force would view Taig's emotional outburst as a sign of divided loyalty, and then Maelin wouldn't be the only guardian they were keeping tabs on.

Taig whipped the dagger out of its holding strap, taking a step toward me. "I'll kill you, Blim!"

My arms moved instinctively, bringing my horse a step forward before I managed to stop myself. *If he wanted to hurt me, he would have drawn his swords.*

"This is *your* fault." With a step back, he laughed even harder, lowering his dagger. "You dragged her into this... into the archives—"

"Go inside, Taig. No one can see you like this."

His false humor faded as he waved his dagger in sporadic sways. "Like *this*? Who do you think *caused* this? You've been encouraging her to act out from the start, and now it's all gone to shit. Do you really hate me so much that you'd ruin her, just to hurt me?"

I froze as a realization struck. Taig had mentioned the archives. He was blaming *me* for this. Clearly whatever happened to Maelin had something to do with her bold opinions. I couldn't shake the feeling that the Meridian book had made her act out during the meeting. And if that were true, then Taig would be right, just like he always was. It would be my fault.

He stopped waving his dagger but continued to glare.

"I don't hate you," I muttered, my eyes stinging.

"Like hell you don't!"

"Tell me where Maelin is."

"So you can kill her?"

"So I can fix this!" I screamed down at him. "Because you clearly can't do *anything* right now!"

My words struck him like a bolt of lightning. His anger melted as he fought off tears, clutching his dagger like it was all he had.

"Where is she?" I yelled.

It took him a second to find his voice. "The Facility," he choked out. "I think she's hurt."

"*Hurt?*"

"They just told me I have the day off. They took my keys. They're making sure I can't get near her."

As I watched him struggle for breaths, I no longer saw the twenty-two-year-old guardian who pinched my nerves. I saw the helpless seventeen-year-old chained to a metal chair, begging for the guardians not to burn him. And this time, instead of believing that he would be okay, I felt the urge to scream and fight like Maelin did. I listened to the faint voice that told me to help.

"Do nothing," I ordered. "I'll talk to Wick."

And with a snap of the reins, I shot off to the Facility.

Goosebumps rose on my arms as I followed Wick through the twisting corridors. Something had always unsettled me about the Facility's silent, night-like darkness while birds were chirping in the daylight outside.

"Wick," I said, fishing for his gaze. "Thanks for this."

He narrowed his eyes, staring directly ahead. "There's no one else I'd do this for."

I sighed. I hated putting him in a position where he felt obligated to choose between duty and friendship, but unfortunately, he was my only shot at speaking with Maelin. *I'll make it up to him someday.*

Wick stopped at a corner, turned around, and pulled a golden stopwatch out of his overcoat. "You have three minutes," he stated firmly, walking past me with a *click*.

As he faded into the darkness we'd come from, I stared at the corner, my blood running cold. Somewhere around it, Maelin had answers I might not want to hear. I clung to the naive hope that her detainment had nothing to do with the Meridian book, and that I could leave the Facility with pure concern, void of guilt. *Please tell me I have nothing to do with this...*

After taking a deep breath, I rounded the corner and entered a dead-end corridor lined with barred holding cells. All I could hear were the echoes of my steps and the flickering of mounted torches as I crept forward, glancing left and right. The cells were empty, their metal beds lined with dusty sheets.

For a moment I feared Wick had led me to the wrong place by accident, or that Maelin had been moved without his knowledge. But then I reached the final cell—the only one that wasn't empty—and froze mid-step.

Behind the bars, Maelin sat on the bed with her knees to her chest, her back to the wall. Bruises marred her face and neck, and blood seeped through her overcoat sleeve around a cut in her forearm. Her puffy, red eyes looked at me, and despite the twitch of her lips, she chose silence.

I swallowed hard, struggling to suppress an explosion of questions. So many of them ran through my head, but one fought its way to my lips first.

"Who hurt you?" I asked, taking a step toward her cell.

"My corrector." Her voice was hardly more than a whisper. "It's not safe here, Blimmery. You need to go."

I took another step and gripped the bars. "*Who?*"

With a sigh, she looked away and offered a name. "Ogga."

I strangled the bars as memories of my shadow unit leader flashed through my mind—taking his meeting notes, laughing at his jokes, listening to his lectures... In an instant, every recollection darkened as I connected alarming details I had previously overlooked.

The *misplaced* notes creased from his pocket, not lost but withheld, then secretly planted on my desk to spark my gratitude in his forgiveness.

His pattern of feigned indignation followed by sudden laughter and praise.

The way he brought a new book into the Office every day, faking an unsustainable reading speed that I innocently admired.

How can I ever forgive myself for believing in a fraud like him?

"That *monster*," I said through gritted teeth.

"You always spoke highly of him." Maelin stood with a wince and limped toward me, her eyes watering. "I-I thought I could trust him." She halted just out of reach, far enough that even if I were to stick my arm between the bars, I couldn't reach her.

"I'm sorry. I didn't know he was violent. I didn't—"

"I'm not blaming you, Blimmery. Trusting him was my decision."

I hesitated. "W-What do you mean by *trusting him*?"

Maelin stepped within reach and leaned in to whisper, "I told him about the Meridian book."

I released the bars like they were aflame, taking a step back. I had thought it went without saying that we would keep the book a secret. *For the glory of Vakoi, that's why we burned it!*

Maelin scoffed. "Now you think I'm crazy too."

"Why would you tell him?"

"What did you expect me to do, Blimmery? Play dumb?"

"*Yes*," I said, raising my voice. "That's exactly what I expected."

"We just found out that the Force is *evil*. To ignore the truth and continue working as usual would make us no better than the guardians behind the sham rebellion. Is that what *you're* planning to do?"

I dodged her question. I didn't have the answer to it.

"Maelin, you're hurt. If you're not careful, they could—they could hurt you even more." My voice shook as I continued. "Please, go along with what they're saying. Just for now, long enough to get you out of here. Once you're back to work, we can process what we read and learn how to live with it."

"*Process* it? Learn how to *live* with it?" Maelin waved her finger at me. "You're saying you want to forget what your uncle wrote. You want to run away. Well, maybe you want a way to *escape* the truth, but I want a way to *expose* it."

"Thanks to Pandora's Box, the truth is spreading."

"You're leaving the work up to an artistic collective? Performers who sell the truth to wealthy people like my patient that end up keeping their mouths shut anyway? Pandora's Box hardly makes a dent. What we need is for guardians in the Force to wake up to the crimes they're committing, and make the truth known to all."

What she wanted was beautiful, but impossible.

"No," I said.

"Blimmery—"

"You're *one person*. You're not going to start a revolution from this cell. Your number one goal should be to convince the guardians to let you go. I promise, once you're back in service, we'll come up with a safer way to spread the truth."

"You're a liar, Blimmery. I saw how easily you led Cove astray, and I'm not falling for the same tricks. I know you're scared. I could feel it last night, and I feel it now. You're not willing to risk your life for this, but I am, and your false promises won't stop me."

"Think about Taig," I jumped in, my speech accelerating. "He's worried sick right now!"

"You can't change my mind. I didn't tell them you were involved. No one recognized us. You can hide all you want, but you can't make me do the same. Standing by the truth, no matter what they do to me, will prove how much I believe what I say. And maybe my resilience will convince them to read the book themselves."

My chest tightened, and I had to gasp to fill my lungs. I had stated facts, made promises, and mentioned Taig. But none of that worked.

"You're wrong," I said. "They'll kill you before they ever believe you. They'll—"

"Blimmery," Wick called from the end of the corridor. "It's time."

"Please, Maelin," I continued, ignoring him. "I'm begging you. Don't do this." I approached the bars again and offered my hand, but she ignored it, looking away.

"Blimmery," Wick called, louder this time.

I swiveled toward him. "One more minute."

"No." Wick marched down the corridor. "There's a unit coming."

"I can't leave her here when she's—"

"Get him out of here, Wick," Maelin said. "Before they lock him up too."

Wick was at my side in an instant, grabbing my upper arm with an iron grip.

"No! I'm not leaving—"

He shoved me into the dead-end wall, my face pressed against the stone and my arm in a tight lock.

"Quiet," he whispered.

Despite the distant footsteps of an approaching unit, I fought against the pain in my elbow, struggling to break free from his grip.

Wick shoved me forward again, applying extra pressure until my eyes were closed and my breaths shook with every exhale. I could nearly taste the stones.

"I'm sorry," Wick added, "but if anyone finds us, we're dead." He released me with a shove, and I winced, stretching my sore elbow.

The unit's footsteps echoed louder as I turned around, my rage settling at the sight of Wick's worried gaze. He was right. We had to leave this corridor before the guardians could spot and trap us. I had already dragged Maelin into danger and couldn't allow myself to do the same to him.

"Go," Maelin said.

Wick led the way down the corridor, trusting that I would follow him. Which I did.

Looking over my shoulder, I held Maelin's gaze until I lost sight of her. That's when something within me snapped, and my emotions cut off. My heart stopped pounding in my ears, my hands stopped sweating, my elbow stopped throbbing... I recalled our lessons at the Academy on staying focused in high-pressure situations, and I did what I had to do without thinking.

As Wick led me through the maze, taking a path to avoid colliding with an approaching unit, I made a mental note of each turn and how many torches we passed between them. *Left, five, right, two, right, six, left, three...*

It took less than a minute for us to lose the sound of the other guardians' footsteps. We had successfully evaded their path on the way to the back door, which Wick had snuck me in through earlier. He unbarred it, and I slipped from the darkness into the blinding sunlight. The salty breeze rustling through my hair, and the warmth against my cheeks were too much for me. My stomach twisted into a knot, the horror striking me all over again.

I faced Wick, my eyes watering as my hands rolled into fists. I couldn't decide whether to thank him for letting me in or punch him for making me leave, so I did neither.

"Please, look out for her," I said, my voice trembling. "You're the only commander here she can trust. Taig was locked out."

"I know." Wick gripped the metal door, the torchlight illuminating his face unevenly. "I made sure of it, for his own sake."

I frowned and tilted my head.

"Tomorrow morning," Wick continued, drawing his words out, "is Maelin's execution."

The ground sunk beneath me as he slammed the door in my face.

Execution?

I jumped to force the door open, but Wick had already barred it, locking me outside.

That can't be!

After a few hopeless shoves at the door, I backed away, tripping over my own feet and falling into a seated position on the grass. A white butterfly flickered angrily around my boots, as if to say, *Maelin will never witness beauty like me again because of you.*

I had told her about Pandora's Box and my desire to read the Meridian book. I had ignored Taig's warning to stop encouraging her when I should have known that he was right. Taig was always right. And for my careless decisions, Maelin was paying the price with her life.

I got her into this mess, I realized, staring up at the Facility's stone wall. *I'm responsible for getting her out.*

My hand acted on its own, reaching into my overcoat for a notebook and pen. All I could think of now was *left, five, right, two...*

I scaled the front steps of the Complex, every step weighing me down. Taig had trusted me to check on Maelin, and what was I returning to tell him? That her execution was scheduled because of me? He would kill me on the spot and scatter my insides across the Complex. I knew that for certain. But I had no choice.

The common room buzzed with its usual liveliness as I entered. A few guardians off service sat on the sofas, laughing together as though nothing was wrong. The gossip about Maelin's operation had died off quickly, and it seemed the recent update about her execution had yet to spread beyond the Facility walls.

I spotted Taig pretending to read in the corner of the room, his boot tapping the floor repeatedly as he peeked over the pages, eavesdropping. When he finally noticed me, he set the book down and ran over.

He didn't ask any questions. He simply stood, waiting.

I opened my mouth, and time seemed to freeze. I scrambled for the right combination of words to break the news, to confess in the softest way possible. I could not lie about something as vital as Maelin's execution.

But despite my efforts, I couldn't manage to speak, so I closed my mouth and offered a look that said, *I'm sorry, Taig. Please forgive me.*

His eyes widened at my hesitation. It was clear, as the panic crossed his face, that he knew his fears had come true.

Without a word, he bolted for the staircase.

I hugged myself and bit my trembling lip, struggling to suppress my visible guilt before the other guardians could notice it. I truly thought I had ruined Taig. He was not an enemy or a friend. He was a fellow graduate, a role model, a brother. I couldn't stand him, but I couldn't stand hating him either. *He's family.*

It dawned on me then, as I recalled our petty arguments over the past six years, that if there was one thing Taig wasn't, it was a coward. He had targeted a more challenging trophy during the final filtration to improve Maelin's chance of success. He had stopped resisting during the branding ceremony to prevent her from pushing the guardians too far. He would do anything for her. And once that clicked, I just *knew* he wasn't going upstairs to sob. He was going upstairs for his swords.

Without stopping once, I raced to our floor, forcing myself into Taig's unlocked flat right as he strapped his primary tool to his back.

"You're not stopping me again!" he shouted, storming toward the hallway. "They're going to kill her!"

I slammed his door behind me and held my arms out, guarding the exit. He tried to shove me aside, but my fist to his jaw sent him stumbling back.

I gasped as he rebounded, unsheathing his sword and pointing it to my chest in a single, sweeping motion. His gritted teeth warned me to run, but instead, I took a step closer, allowing his tool to graze my vest.

"This isn't the way." I grabbed the cold, sharp blade with my trembling hand. "We can still save Maelin, but we need a plan."

Taig's lips twitched as I guided the sword away from my chest. He kept it raised when I released it, but he didn't aim at me again.

Please, don't ask me why I care. I raised my palms in surrender. *Don't make me confess that I'm guilty. Just let me help you.*

A painful silence passed before he finally spoke, his voice breaking.

"You'd really do this for me?"

I forced a weak smile. "Why *wouldn't* I help you? We graduated together."

The ferocity in his eyes softened, just a little.

"Okay, Blimmery." Taig sheathed his sword. "What's the plan?"

CHAPTER 10

CORRECTOR

The fattest lie fed to us as children is that the world is evil,
and that we require protection from the people who make it so.

♫ DEAD OF DAY - KOETHE ♫

I'll never know *exactly* what happened during Maelin's third correctional meeting. I can only rely on the word of the commander who guarded the Facility's front door that morning, another guardian who overheard her conversation with Wick in the corridors, and the transcript Kanter read to me after she died.

But with these sources, and a few educated guesses, I've constructed a narrative that I believe aligns closely with Maelin's true experiences and mindset during the events that unfolded.

It all began at 7:50, when she arrived at the Facility ten minutes early for her meeting. According to the commander at the front door, her uniform was wrinkly, clearly not a freshly pressed set, and her eyes and lips were dark and blemished.

"Doctor Maelin!" the commander exclaimed. "Are you hurt?"

"No," she said, unstrapping her bow and quiver of arrows. "Here's my primary tool." She thrust them into the commander's grip and stepped toward the door, but he held his arm out, stopping her.

"What's with the attitude this morning?"

Maelin glued her lips shut.

"Secondary tool," the commander demanded, holding a palm out.

With a bored expression, she retrieved the dagger from her overcoat and handed it to him. "Would you like my *tertiary* tool too?"

He held the door open. "Get inside before I tell your corrector about this."

When Maelin stormed into the building, the commander slammed the metal door behind her. She scoffed and headed for the correctional meeting room, mounted torches crackling with a satisfying rage as she zoomed through the corridors.

"Back—"

Maelin gasped, reaching instinctively for a quiver of arrows she no longer had.

"Back for more?" Wick appeared beside her as though materializing from the shadows. "Third day in a row. You must like this place."

Maelin settled her breath, refusing to look at him as their steps fell in sync. "Trust me, I'd rather be anywhere else."

"Are you sure? Apart from a few hours a day, you get a full week off service!"

Maelin chuckled bitterly. "The free time isn't worth doing stupid homework assignments for." She handed Wick a folded page, and after skimming it, he burst into laughter.

"The old man made you write about *every* time a guardian pricked your nerves? Oh, this is golden!"

"It's not funny. He's trying to humiliate me."

"It's working, and it's hilarious."

She snatched the page. "Hand me a pen so I can add this moment to the list."

"Woah, woah!" Wick held his palms up. "I'm just trying to lighten the mood."

Maelin finally looked at him, and his eyes widened. "I get it, Wick. I'm just... not feeling very bright this morning."

His voice deepened. "You're not looking too bright either. Why's your face all bruised?"

"It's just makeup. Couldn't get it to wash off." She rubbed her eyelids with her sleeve.

"Since when do you wear makeup?" Wick asked. After a moment without a reply, he shook his head. "Never mind. Just take it easy, okay? All you need to do is get through this week, and your life will go back to normal." He gave her arm a gentle touch and vanished into the shadows.

Maelin's grip on the paper tightened as she stepped into the correctional meeting room, which sharply contrasted the rest of the Facility with its white walls and numerous hanging lanterns to brighten the space. The only furniture inside were two sofas facing each other and a short mahogany table between them. Frames on the walls featured nearly identical abstract paintings.

Maelin sat on one of the sofas and slammed her homework onto the table. The last thing she wanted was to talk to that self-righteous professor again, especially now that she knew about the Force's hidden agenda.

The door opened, and a young professor with wild, unnatural red hair dragged himself in. His disheveled uniform and sloppy footsteps contrasted the elegance of the correctional meeting room and the refined image of the Force in general. She recognized him as Ogga, Kanter's unit leader.

"Good morning, Doctor Maelin. You look surprised to see me," Ogga observed, a touch of humor in his tone. "I've been assigned to replace your last corrector for the remainder of the week."

"And why is that?" Maelin asked.

Ogga shrugged, though his smirk implied that he knew the answer.

When he sat on the sofa across from her, the door swung open again to welcome Kanter, who offered Maelin an awkward smile. She couldn't tell if he recognized her from Pandora's Ball, but regardless, the corners of her lips twitched upward. *It'll be nice to have a friendly face around*, she thought.

Kanter rushed to join Ogga on the sofa, pulling a notebook and pen out of his overcoat.

"Lengthy," Ogga said, snatching Maelin's homework assignment from the table. "These are all the times you've been frustrated at a guardian?"

"The main ones," Maelin muttered, squinting at his youthful face. Did the guardians truly believe that a man just four years older than her was a better fit to correct her mind than the white-bearded professor?

Kanter bit his lip, transcribing their conversation into his notebook.

"So..." Ogga's eyes hopped around the page until he settled on an event to focus on. "During the branding ceremony, you lashed out at the Academy guardians because they wouldn't mark you first. Walk me through that, will you?"

Maelin leaned forward. "It's self-explanatory, Professor, but sure, I'll hold your hand."

Kanter pursed his lips to conceal a grin.

"Okay." Ogga leaned forward, mirroring her. "Hold my hand."

Maelin straightened and crossed her arms. "Taig's afraid of getting burned."

"That's quite odd for a tough guy like him. What's the story there?"

"A stupid incident at Frontal Orphanage."

With a smirk, Ogga propped his chin on his hand. "Do tell."

"It's a long story."

"We have three hours."

"Fine," Maelin snapped, a bit harsher than she'd intended. "We had a rat infestation in the building. There was a girl who made a habit of luring them into jars and trapping them, just to watch them choke and die."

"As kids do," Ogga said.

Maelin frowned. "Excuse me?"

"It was a joke. Go on."

Maelin looked away and took a deep breath. "One night, during supper, I confronted her about it. We were yelling back and forth, and she ended up chucking her soup at me. It was piping hot, right from the kitchen. But Taig stepped over and took the hit."

"So Commander Taig is a hero," Ogga said slowly, "for protecting you from *soup*?"

"It left a scar on his stomach." Maelin raised her voice. "That soup would have burned my face. It could've blinded me!"

"And?" Ogga replied, as though she had made no point at all. "I understand that Taig's act of *bravery* resulted in a fear of getting burned, but we're talking about the ceremony here. Why did the order of branding bother you so much? Even if you swapped places and went first, Taig would have faced his fear eventually. He'd still end up with a mark."

"That's not the point," Maelin argued. "I wasn't trying to prevent his branding. I was trying to ease him into it. The ceremony would have been awful regardless, but seeing the process upfront would have helped him handle it."

"You don't know that."

"Yes, I do. Because I *know* Taig. And the Academy guardians *know* that I know him, but they didn't let me call the shot. Commander Blank held me back. They could have easily changed the order, but they didn't."

"Why do you think they marked him first, despite your request?"

"They wanted to send us a message."

"And that message is..."

"That they own us."

Ogga rubbed his chin, his lips downturned in what appeared to be a forced expression of sympathy. "What a depressing way to live, that must be. I'm saddened to hear that you believe the Force, your family, would put you through emotional turmoil to send a cruel message like that."

"It should be depressing for all of us because it's the truth," Maelin said. "The Force is controlling us like puppets to pull off the Royal Family's master plan."

"It sounds like someone convinced you of a conspiracy theory. Why don't you share it with me, so we can discuss its feasibility together?"

Maelin closed her mouth. *No. I can't say it.* To mention the Meridian book would be an admission of treason. Perhaps it was time to finally take Taig's advice and think before speaking her mind.

"Is something wrong?" Ogga said, raising a brow.

Kanter stopped writing and looked up from his notebook. Maelin couldn't read his blank expression, but the fact that he caught her gaze felt like a warning.

"It's nothing." Her eyes darted to the door.

"Don't be afraid." Ogga leaned back, sinking comfortably into the sofa.

"I'm just looking to have an open conversation with a fellow guardian."

"Right," Maelin said.

"You seem skeptical. Perhaps it'll ease your mind to know that we're here to sort through your thoughts, not to punish you. So feel free to sit for a while, and once you're ready, I'll be thrilled to hear what you think the Royal Family's *master plan* is."

The scribbling of Kanter's pen against the page filled the air as Maelin analyzed Ogga's smug expression. As conceited as the man was, he looked genuinely interested in her perspective. Blimmery had told her, a couple of years prior, that he'd shadowed Ogga during the second half of the program and admired his intellect. *Maybe there's a chance Professor Ogga would listen to my story, and consider the facts.*

Kanter stopped writing, meeting Maelin's gaze again with a subtle shake of his head.

Everyone's always trying to silence me. Maelin folded her hands in her lap, her fingers strangling each other. *At what point do I trust the guardians enough to spread the truth? If no one speaks up, nothing will change.*

With a sigh, Maelin relaxed her hands. "Emperor Vakoi created a fake rebel faction." She paused, observing Ogga's response to determine if it was safe to say more.

Ogga turned to Kanter, who stared at Maelin with wide eyes.

"Go on," Ogga whispered, nudging his side. "Write it down."

Kanter lowered his head, his hand shaking as he wrote.

Ogga watched his unit member for a few seconds before returning his focus to Maelin. "By rebel faction, are you referring to the Underground?"

"Yes." Maelin leaned forward. "It isn't rebels from the Atherus Empire who are vandalizing our property, looting our markets, or distributing drugs and counterfeit coins. It's us. A small group of guardians sworn to secrecy is coordinating disturbances to place the blame on Emperor Atherus' people. Then, a larger group of guardians—that's us—unknowingly cleans up the mess."

Ogga chuckled. "And what would the point of that be?"

"For the Prince to dominate the entire island," Maelin explained. "If Emperor Vakoi seizes the Atherus Empire now, our people would be furious.

No one wants a power-hungry leader and a pointless war. But if he stages disturbances over a long period of time, and blames them on the other side, our people will eventually beg the Force to take down the Atherus Empire. It's all part of a slow, thirty-year plan to ensure that Emperor Vakoi's son will have complete control after he takes power. And we're already twelve years into it."

"Wow. What a creative and... *specific* theory," Ogga said. "It must have taken some time to put that together."

"I didn't put it together."

A flicker of concern crossed Ogga's face before he masked it with a smile. "Then who did?"

Maelin narrowed her eyes, her voice deepening. "I read the Meridian book."

Ogga's smile vanished, and Kanter stopped writing, his arm going tense. The room seemed to darken, but Maelin didn't allow the mood to dampen her spirit. She had caught Ogga off-guard and snatched his full attention —now was the perfect time to nail her point.

Today, I'm the corrector, not the other way around.

"The Royal Family is playing a dangerous game with innocent people. They're planning well poisonings and violent raids on our own towns, and for what? A bit of land? Resources? We can't let them get away with this. If we spread the truth among guardians, we could prevent so much suffering."

"Are you hearing yourself?" Ogga asked. "Do you realize how crazy you sound?"

"I'm sick of hearing that." Maelin stood and glared down at him. "I'm *not* crazy. I know that now."

Ogga jumped to his feet, his hand striking Maelin's face before she could blink. Her cheek stung as she raised a palm to shield it.

"Professor," Kanter warned.

"Keep writing," Ogga said.

Maelin breathed heavily, resisting the urge to strike him back. *I need to stay calm. Maybe part of him believes me, and he's overreacting because he's afraid of the truth.* She lowered her arm, forcing herself to meet his gaze again.

"Listen, Professor," she said, speaking more softly this time. "I wouldn't believe Meridian blindly, but everything he wrote about the Force lines up with what I've seen myself. The way the guardians didn't care about Taig, or my patient, or me... It's easy to believe that some seek power and control at the cost of their humanity."

"We're not evil," Ogga spat, his face turning red.

"Think about it. Meridian recognized a guardian who writes for *Capital Weekly* among a group of so-called Underground thieves. He could have ignored what he saw, but instead, he risked everything to uncover the truth and share it with us. And how do we repay him? By *killing* him and banning his book of truth? How is that not evil?"

Ogga took a deep breath, the redness dissipating as he calmed himself. "You listen to *me*, Maelin," he said, his tone patronizing. "I read a lot of books. A lot more than you. Some are good, some are bad, and some are evil. And the evil ones, Maelin, are the only ones I choose *not* to read. You see, books are not *just books*. They're doors into the author's imagination. If the author's imagination is dangerous, then sharing that door with the public is irresponsible."

"It's not censored because it's dangerous, *Ogga*!" Maelin shouted, dropping his honorific. "It's censored because it's true!"

He struck her across the face again, hard enough that she gasped.

"That's enough!" Kanter yelled, but Ogga didn't listen. He stepped onto the table and shoved Maelin to the sofa.

Maelin had no time to process what was happening before he was on top of her, a fist striking her face, splitting her lip against her teeth. Bitter blood trailed along her tongue as she stared him in the eye, refusing to look away.

"You're not supposed to hurt her," Kanter said, his voice less bold and more like a plea. "This isn't physical correction."

"It is now," Ogga said, and struck her again.

Maelin shut her eyes, an ache spreading through her face. Her pulse quickened as she finally pushed back, but the dagger trailing against the fabric of her overcoat sleeve made her freeze.

"Don't move," Ogga warned.

Maelin's body ran cold.

"Say it," he added.

"Say what?"

"Say that you're wrong."

Maelin's voice shook. "Do you really think that by hurting me, you'll change what I know?"

He grabbed her by the collar, pulling her to her feet. "Say that you're wrong," he repeated.

"I can't lie to you."

"Everything you've said is a lie." Ogga's voice was empty, heartless. And it struck Maelin, as the dagger punctured her sleeve and drew blood, that he would never believe her.

I need to get out of here.

Despite the pain in her arm, she pulled him toward her, jamming her elbow into his windpipe. He clenched his neck, the dagger slipping from his grip and clattering against the floor.

Maelin dove for the tool, grabbing it while Ogga was still struggling for his breath. She pivoted with a grunt and jammed the blade into his arm deeper than he'd stabbed her.

Ogga wailed, his eyes clenched shut as he unsheathed one of his swords. Maelin yanked the blade out of his arm as she backed away.

With labored breaths, Ogga opened his eyes and glanced at the cut in his overcoat sleeve, which was beginning to ooze with blood. He slowly raised his sword.

"Stop," Kanter said, his face pale.

As Ogga inched forward, Maelin stepped back. A single swing was all it would take for him to kill her, and considering how he'd broken Protocol by hurting her, she couldn't trust that he wouldn't end her life too.

After a few more steps, Ogga stopped. His shoulders loosened as he changed directions and walked backward toward the door.

"Watch her," he ordered Kanter, sheathing his sword.

Maelin gripped her bleeding arm, her eyes watering as Ogga left the room and shut the door behind him. The wall muffled his shouts from the corridor, but it was clear he was calling a unit for help.

Kanter eyed Ogga's bloody dagger in Maelin's grip, creeping toward her with his palms raised. She took a step back anyway.

"I'm sorry," Kanter said, his voice shaking. "I should have stopped him. I should have—"

"It's okay," Maelin said, taking another step back. "It's not your fault. Ogga broke Protocol. He won't get away with this."

Kanter halted, his eyes watering too. "You have no idea how much he gets away with."

As he finished that statement, the door burst open, and a Defense unit stormed inside with their primary tools drawn.

"Maelin claims to have read the Meridian book." Ogga emerged from behind them, clutching his bleeding arm. "Now she's gonna tell us how she got her hands on a copy."

The horrified look on Kanter's face told Maelin that Ogga had lied, that he had told these commanders she had stolen his dagger and attacked him first. Her only way to regain the Force's trust would be to turn on Blimmery and Pandora's Box.

Only a small number know the truth, and I refuse to expose them.

"Who gave you a copy?" Ogga shouted.

She said nothing.

"Tell them what they want," Kanter whispered. "I'll find a way to help you." His promise was generous, but still, she pursed her lips.

It was less than a minute later when the guardians dragged Maelin out of the bright meeting room and into the dreary Facility corridors.

CHAPTER 11

KILLER

In a society where trust is the rarest and most volatile currency,
betrayal stains even the firmest of handshakes.

♫ OVER THE HILL · WAX//WANE ♫

Red. The color flickered through the inky air as I held another match to the old, wooden structure. An innocent glow marked the window frame —which I'd drenched in lantern oil—and soon morphed into a furious scarlet patch that matched the others, warming my hands.

"Blim!" Taig called from the road behind me, keeping his distance. "That's enough!"

I tucked the matchbox into my overcoat and walked backward, emptying the jar of oil onto the creaking porch steps before chucking it aside. The glass shattered against the road as I gazed up at the restaurant. Thin smoke lines decorated the air around it, swirling upward toward the moon. It wouldn't take long to draw attention from the commanders stationed at the Detainment Facility a few minutes' horse ride away.

"Blim," Taig called again, his voice deeper now. "We need to go."

I turned my back on the building and jogged to Taig, who led me through the narrow woods separating the commercial block from the Detainment Facility. I was winded by the time we emerged from the trees and hid around the corner from the Facility's front door.

With my back to the stone wall, I gazed at the stars and focused on suppressing my heavy breaths. *There's no turning back now.*

I flinched at the sound of the creaking front door. Taig reached over his shoulders to grip the handles of his dual swords.

"Commander!" a guardian yelled into the Facility. "I think there's a fire!" Protocol forbade him from abandoning his post, so he couldn't investigate the smoke himself, nor could he enter the building and track his unit down.

It took a few minutes for the two commanders inside to hear his calls and emerge from the Facility. They mumbled between each other, discussing the smoke, before unlocking the stable and riding their horses toward the blazing restaurant, leaving the guardian who had called them behind at his post.

Once the sound of the horses' hooves clip-clopping in the woods faded, Taig unsheathed his swords and bolted from our hiding spot. I peered around the corner right as he reeled his primary tool back.

"Taig?" The commander jumped aside, dodging Taig's oncoming strike, and drew his own swords. "What the hell are you doing?"

Without answering, Taig darted after the commander again. The clashing of their tools cut through the night as I whipped out my dagger and waited. It didn't take long for Taig to slip past an attack and bash the guardian's skull with his blunt sword handle.

The commander staggered, and I swooped in from behind, landing a second hit to his head with my dagger handle. The impact threw him to the ground, his eyes clenched shut. Streaks of blood trailed down his forehead.

Taig and I held our positions, ready to keep fighting, but after a few groans, the commander stilled.

My eyes widened. *Our plan was to knock him out, not kill him.*

I stashed my dagger and knelt to check the commander's pulse, but Taig's nonchalant tone interrupted me.

"If he dies, he dies, Blim."

I studied the injured commander's face, hesitating to stand. "How long will the fire distract them?"

"I don't care." Taig sheathed his swords and swung the door open. The Facility's darkness devoured him when he stepped inside, vanishing into a space blacker than the air I knelt in.

I shot the commander a final look before standing and wiping my palms on my pants. Part of me didn't want to know if my blow had killed him anyway.

As I crept toward the open door, it seemed to mock me, saying, *Enter the void, Blimmery, and you might never make it out.*

"Hurry up!" Taig called from inside.

After taking a deep breath, I joined him in the foyer.

"Let's bar them out." Taig slammed the door behind me and slid a metal bar into place, ensuring the commanders who had left couldn't reenter. "What section is she in?"

"I don't know the terminology."

"Dammit, Blim! We memorized the floor plan."

"Yes, *four years ago*. We're not trainees anymore." I pulled my notebook out. "But relax. I can find her from the back door."

Taig scanned my page of directions with a chuckle. "How pathetic. Follow me."

He moved swiftly through the corridors, his back-strapped swords glistening in the torchlight. In less than a minute, we reached the back door and verified that it was also barred, just in case. Then I followed my notebook's directions to guide us. *Right turn, pass four torches, left turn, pass three torches, left turn, pass six torches...*

As I led the way, my chest tightened at the thought of seeing Maelin behind bars again. *If only I had never told her about Pandora's Box. If only I had never asked Kanter to let me into the archives. If only I had never pestered Doctor Rem to tell me what happened during the operation incident. I could have lived in ignorance, and Maelin could have avoided the death penalty.*

I lost my sense of direction and referred to my notebook again. *Snap out of it, Blimmery. You messed up, but you're here to fix that.*

We turned the final corner and walked down the dead-end corridor, stopping in unison at Maelin's cell. She lay sideways on the bed, her chest rising and falling in uneven patterns, her face sweaty and more bruised than earlier.

"Mae!" Taig sprang forward and gripped the bars.

Maelin swayed as she sat up, revealing her strikingly small pupils.

My jaw tightened. *They drugged her.* The symptoms pointed to an injection of calabar, known for its truth-telling capabilities in small doses. *Even with her execution scheduled, they still attempted to wring information out of her.*

"Mae," Taig repeated, softer this time.

Her pupils expanded slightly as she focused on us, and with a shake of her head, she croaked, "Leave."

"No. We're here to free you." Taig nodded at me, and I pulled out my lock busters. My hands shook as I inserted the tension wrench and pick into the cell's keyhole.

"We'll go somewhere far, Mae. We'll hide in the Atherus Empire, where the Force can't trace us."

I scrambled with my tools, trying to locate and unlatch the binding pin. *Why isn't it working?* I'd busted hundreds of locks in training, but none of them had ever been this difficult.

"We can start a new life there," Taig continued. "We did it once, and we can do it again."

When Maelin sniffled, I froze, looking up as a few tears fell. "I've already accepted this." She wiped her cheek. "You need to go."

"No!" Taig and I shouted in unison. I refocused on the keyhole and bit my lip, applying more pressure to my tools. Never before had I seen Maelin give up like this. It couldn't be her. I needed to bust this lock and bring the real Maelin back.

"Blimmery, stop that. I already tried."

My hands fumbled, and I looked up again. Maelin pointed to the floor of her cell, where her own lock busters were lying. The guardians hadn't confiscated hers because the tools wouldn't work anyway.

Taig snatched my lock busters and shoved me out of the way. His hands shook more than mine as he moved the wrench and pick with no rhyme or reason. The door refused to budge.

I stepped toward him. "We need to—"

Taig threw my lock busters down and pulled out his own, as if those would work any better.

"We need to stay calm," I warned him.

A few tense seconds of his tinkering passed before he tossed his lock busters down too.

Maelin backed away as Taig unsheathed his swords and aimed at the cell. I gripped his arm in protest, but he shook me off and swung the blades down. They grated against the bars with a metallic scream, forcing Maelin and me to cover our ears with our hands.

"You can't free me without a key," Maelin stated.

Taig gripped his sword handles tighter. "Then I'll get a damn key!"

"No. Listen, you can't..."

As Maelin argued with him, a clinking in the distance distracted me. I closed my eyes, tuning into the sound of a sliding metal bar. It had come from the direction of the main entrance. But how could someone unbar the front door from outside?

They couldn't, which means...

"Taig," I muttered, "we're not alone." One of the commanders had stayed behind, and we had locked ourselves in with them.

Despite my warning, Taig scraped his swords against the bars again, so loudly I was certain the guardian by the front door could hear. That's when the weight of my crimes struck me at full force.

My breaths clotted my throat. I had lied to Cove, broken a Vow, and purchased the Meridian book. I had committed arson, knocked out—possibly murdered—a commander, and snuck into the Facility. In the past few days, I had morphed from a guardian into a traitor.

If I couldn't calm Taig down, the Force would discover everything I had done. *And they'll kill me like they killed Uncle Meridian.*

I lurched forward and wrapped my arms around Taig's waist, trying to haul him back while Maelin whispered fiercely for him to be quiet.

But I wasn't strong enough, and Maelin wasn't convincing enough.

Taig only stopped when a guardian emerged in the corridor, dual swords drawn and face masked by the shadows.

As the figure inched toward us, I plucked a star from my bandolier. *This could be a blessing in disguise. If we defeat this guardian, we can steal his keys to get Maelin out.*

The commander halted by a mounted torch, illuminating his face. "I should have known you were planning something."

I exhaled, a bit of tension leaving my shoulders. Of all the guardians who could have confronted us, thankfully, it was Wick. He had broken the rules to help me once, so perhaps I could convince him to do so again.

Wick's eyes darted from Taig to Maelin, and finally, to the picks and wrenches scattered about the floor. He let out a long breath and lowered his primary tool. "Where would you bring her?"

Taig kept his swords raised. "Anywhere but here."

Wick sent me a look that said, *I understand why you're doing this, but you need to stop.*

"Please, Wick. Let us free her." I returned the star to my bandolier. "You can say you were ambushed and had your keys stolen. The Force won't blame you a bit."

"You know she doesn't deserve this," said Taig.

"If that's too risky, I understand," said Maelin, a bit of hope seeping into her voice. "But please, whatever you choose, don't tell anyone that Taig and Blimmery were here."

Wick gulped as he faced her cell. "I'm so sorry, Maelin. But... I don't have your key."

"What?" I whispered.

Maelin smiled weakly at Wick. "It's okay," she whispered.

Wick turned back to Taig and me, his eyes watering. "You're right. She doesn't deserve this, and it's awful, but there's nothing any of us can do. So please, take your lock busters and get out of here before my unit returns. I won't say a word."

I shook my head, my knees buckling. After everything we had done to get here, I couldn't allow our plan to fail. There had to be a way to free Maelin without a key. *Think, Blimmery!*

Taig took a step forward. "Say it to her face."

Wick backed up, keeping his distance. "Say *what*?"

"Tell Maelin that you want her dead."

"No." Wick frowned and raised his voice. "That's not true!"

Taig charged at him, forcing Wick to stumble back and redraw his swords.

"Stop!" Maelin yelled.

By the time Wick blocked the attack, Taig's blades were only inches from cutting into his shoulders.

"You liar!" Taig shouted into his face. "I know you have her key!"

"I don't!" Wick yelled, retaliating with a combination.

"Taig, listen to him," Maelin pleaded. "Wick's been the only one nice to me. He brought me food. He's done nothing but care."

Wick crossed his blades, locking Taig's swords at their intersection. His kick sent Taig staggering, and in that moment of weakness, Wick rushed after him with a sword swing that he barely deflected.

I stepped closer. "Wick! You could kill him!"

"*He'll* kill *me*!" Wick argued.

"Not if you give me her key," Taig grumbled.

Maelin stomped her boots and shouted, "He doesn't have it, Taig!"

I reached for my dagger, nearing them as the clashing of steel rang out at faster intervals. If anyone had the combat skills to avoid bloodshed and still get what he wanted, it was Taig—but there was something off about him tonight. His movements lacked his usual elegance and strategy. I had a feeling he wouldn't win without bloodshed—and an even stronger feeling he wouldn't win at all.

As Maelin pleaded for them to stop, Wick's blade arched toward the crown of Taig's head, threatening a fatal blow that couldn't be blocked in time.

I didn't want to choose between two brothers that night, but the clock was ticking, so I lunged—and my dagger found its mark.

With a twist of my wrist, and the sound of squelching flesh, time seemed to halt. Swords stopped clashing. Maelin stopped shouting.

And Wick started bleeding.

He toppled into the wall, his eyes widening as he stared down at my dagger in his chest. It had pierced him at a downward angle, right above the edge of his armored vest.

"Why?" he murmured, looking up at me.

I diverted my gaze, bile rising in my throat. I had stabbed Wick to spare Maelin the pain of witnessing the person she trusted most die during what could be the final hours of her life. But in sparing her heart, and saving Taig's life, I had done something unforgivable.

Wick choked for air that refused to enter his lungs, either due to shock or his leaking wound. I wasn't sure.

All I knew was that I couldn't handle what I'd done.

I turned my back on Wick, but even the sound of his body hitting the floor behind me was too much to bear. My eyes burned as Maelin's face contorted. She doubled over, hands on her face, sobs overtaking her. My effort to spare her heart had ruined her anyway.

What the hell have I done?

My head jerked forward as I vomited, tears violently splattering from my eyes. Wick had made me strong when I was weak, and I had let him be weak when he wasn't strong. But after everything we had persevered through together, my dagger had transformed me from his brother into his killer. He didn't deserve this. The blade belonged in *my* chest, not his.

It felt like a lifetime that I stood hunched over, sobbing and taking in the stench of my vomit, before Taig sheathed his swords. He set a warm hand on my shoulder.

"Get a hold of yourself, Blim," he ordered, but there was a softness in his tone.

I wiped my cheeks and lips with my sleeve, fighting emotions that clawed for every ounce of my attention.

Taig's hand left my shoulder. My back was still turned, but I heard him snatch a jingling key ring from Wick's overcoat. He tested them on Maelin's door, one by one. They clearly didn't work, because in about a minute, the keys clinked against the floor, and Taig threw curses into the air.

"That's enough!" Maelin said, cutting him off. "If you don't leave now, they'll kill all three of us."

But even if we were to leave without Maelin, the commander at the front door had seen Taig. *We need to make sure he's dead.* The idea had struck me without welcome, and I wished it had come from someone else. Just minutes ago, I had been worried for that man's life.

What has become of me?

I refused to be a monster. I rejected the identity. I turned around and knelt by Wick's body.

I checked his pulse.

Nothing.

I rested my ear against his bleeding chest.

Nothing.

I shook my head and clutched his warm hand, refusing to believe it. Another surge of bile threatened to rise, but the echoes of distant footsteps scared my nausea away. I recalled how Wick had unbarred the front door, and I dropped his lifeless hand.

The commanders are back.

"You need to go," Maelin said.

Taig didn't argue this time. He simply walked around me and dismounted two torches from the wall, taking them into his steady hands. He didn't flinch, even with the fire close to his skin.

"Taig," Maelin warned. "Don't. They'll kill you. They'll—"

Without looking at her, Taig raced down the corridor with the flames in his grip and disappeared around the corner.

Maelin covered her mouth with her hands, muting a scream.

He's going to fight them, and he can't possibly win. I gulped a bitter taste and listened for his footsteps, but they were soundless. I couldn't hear him. It was like Taig had disappeared for good.

"Blimmery," Maelin said. "You need to leave alone."

I stared at the floor.

"Come here," she added. "Please."

After a few seconds, I stood at Wick's side and slowly faced Maelin. She reached through the bars, her hands finding mine. They were so cold. Even colder than Wick's.

"You're letting them kill you," I said, my voice breaking.

"This isn't me giving up, okay? This is me fighting." Maelin squeezed my hands tighter. "They tried everything, but I didn't tell them how I got that book. If you leave now, no one will ever suspect you were part of this. With your knowledge, you can make a change from inside the Force."

I cried, clutching her hands and pressing my forehead to the bars. Even after everything I'd done, Maelin trusted me, but I didn't have the strength to trust myself. I couldn't do what she wanted. If she couldn't, how could I?

"I'm not a writer, Blimmery," Maelin said, as though she could read my mind. "I can't say things in a way that makes people listen. But you know how to tell a good story. People all over the Empire read your articles. You have more power than you believe."

I closed my eyes and whispered, "No."

"I'm suffering, no matter what. The execution is scheduled. I can't leave this cell. So please, be kind to me, do one thing right tonight, and let me go. *Live*, so you can write the truth." She squeezed my hands for the last time and released me.

I reached through the bars for her, but she stepped out of range.

Withdrawing my hand, I contemplated her request. Living in the aftermath of a disaster like this would be crueler than death. She asked too much of me, but I owed it to her, because I was standing on the safe side of the bars, and she was standing on the other.

Okay, Maelin. The words were a mere whisper in my heart. *I'll write the truth.*

"Go," she said, and I ran as fast as my legs could carry me, retracing my path in a frantic dash. *Left, five, right, two...*

As I turned one of the corners, I spotted Taig through an entryway in the corridor as he chucked torches at the commanders. I called his name, but he didn't hear me, and the guardians that he raced after, screaming, likely didn't hear me either.

The ruckus faded as I continued to the back door, unbarred it, and stepped into the air that smoke from my fire had muddled.

And like a ghost, I disappeared into the night.

CHAPTER 12

WRITER

The best fighters are not those who rush into combat
but those who dwell quietly in the shadows, waiting to strike.

♫ RED - MT. WOLF ♫

I might have spent close to two hours in the shower, scrubbing myself with a fresh bar of soap until only half of it remained. That's when I realized my efforts would never cleanse my sins, and sat myself on the tile floor. The stream of water dragged my hair down to cover my eyes, and in the darkness, I imagined myself drowning in the ocean.

Did Taig survive the fight? The sound of splattering water faded, and all I could hear were the echoing thoughts in my head. *What did the guardians do with Wick's body? Did they execute Maelin yet?*

My fingers were soggy and wrinkled by the time I left the shower. I dried myself, shaved my face, and brushed my teeth. I changed into a fresh uniform and strapped my bandolier of throwing blades across my chest. I prepared for the morning as though I hadn't murdered Wick Saratoga.

I made my bed, picked up my laundry, washed my dishes, and tidied my closet. I even reorganized my shelf of books in alphabetical order, then by color, and finally, by favorite to least favorite. Then back to alphabetical order. *I don't deserve to play favorites.*

For the next few hours, I sat on the cold floor and listened for footsteps from the hallway. I waited for Taig to come home.

The warmth of dawn had yet to meet my curtains when a guardian unit's hammering footsteps interrupted the silence.

"Everyone up! Everyone up!" the unit yelled on their way upstairs, stirring guardians from slumber on every floor. "Emergency assembly at the Facility!"

My pulse quickened as their voices grew louder. *This is it.* I stood and backed away from the door. *My last moment of freedom. They're here to bust the lock to my flat and capture me like the traitor I am.*

Nearby doors creaked open, followed by my floormates muttering in the hallway.

"What's going on?"

"It's too early for this..."

"I bet it's about Maelin's operation."

"Seems worse than that."

I flinched when someone pounded on my door.

"Blimmery!" Kanter shouted. "Wake up!"

My eyes widened, and I reached for my bandolier. *They sent Kanter to capture me.*

He pounded on the door again. "Are you in there?"

I released a star, leaving the tool in its holding strap. Kanter's voice had turned quiet and raspy, twinged with desperation. *He's not here to capture me.*

After taking a few seconds to gather my courage, I stepped forward and unlocked the door.

"Blimmery," Kanter said, furrowing his brows at my polished appearance. He had clearly just woken up, his collars unfolded and his hair unbrushed.

"Everyone up!" the unit continued to call. "Emergency assembly!"

Guardians marched behind Kanter on their way to the staircase, their voices a blur of groggy confusion.

"Let's go," Kanter said, gesturing for me to follow.

I joined him in the hallway and locked the door to my flat. *The Force hasn't caught me yet, but surely the guardians at the Facility know what I've done by now. My freedom will soon be over.*

As we followed our floormates, my steps felt mechanical. I was the only guardian here who knew the truth about what had transpired last night—who knew I had killed Wick and abandoned Maelin and Taig. I was surrounded by family, but so, so alone.

Kanter leaned toward me and whispered, "They're not here."

I stared directly ahead without a word, knowing he was referring to Maelin, Taig, and Wick. *He must have knocked on their doors too.*

But unlike me, they hadn't answered.

By 6:00 in the morning, almost all of the hundred guardians had gathered in the Detainment Facility's foyer, where numerous arched entryways led into corridors. My gaze drifted through the darkness of the entryway Taig and I had entered last night, the image of my knife in Wick's body flashing through my mind.

I stared at my boots, battling another wave of nausea.

Kanter set a hand on my shoulder, and I closed my eyes and swallowed hard. *Stop acting strange, Blimmery. You'll make him suspicious.*

"Attention, guardians!"

The mumbling trailed off as Kanter let go of me. I looked up to see Commander Blank enter the foyer from one of the corridors.

"We have called you here this morning," Commander Blank continued, "to announce the solemn events of last night."

I clenched my fists at my sides, preparing for him to make eye contact with me—but he didn't.

"As I'm sure you've all heard by now, Doctor Maelin Vandros of Frontal was assigned to a week of mental correctional meetings after an incident at Vakoi City Hospital. She wasn't particularly open-minded during those meetings, and yesterday, the situation escalated when she stabbed her corrector, Professor Ogga Marrow of Miranda, in the forearm."

I shook my head. Maelin had confessed to telling Ogga about the Meridian book, but she had never mentioned attacking him. *That doesn't sound like her.*

I scanned the crowd of stunned guardians, but Ogga wasn't among us. Kanter appeared to be looking for him too, his face reddening as though the news outraged him more than it shocked him. I wouldn't find out, until a few weeks later, that Kanter had been there during that meeting.

Commander Blank cleared his throat, drawing our attention back to him. "Last night, one of Maelin's fellow graduates, Commander Taig Bitterview of Frontal, started a fire to distract the Defense unit at the Facility. His attempt to break her out resulted in the injury of two guardians, who are currently in treatment at the Hospital, and the tragic death of Commander Wick Saratoga of Nominner. Taig was killed to prevent further harm."

Some guardians cursed. Others sniffled.

But I simply froze. I had spent the night clinging to the hope that if Taig didn't return to the Complex, that meant the guardians had captured him. They would interrogate him, beat him up, drug him, but they wouldn't *kill* him. That was too much. That was impossible.

"No..." Kanter whispered.

I thought back to my petty disagreements with Taig over the years. Maelin had told me once, that if we had met anywhere else, we could have been friends. It was only now, as I longed to see Taig's face more than anything, that I believed her.

"In light of these events, the Force assembled us here to witness a ceremony initially intended to be private—Maelin's execution."

I gasped. *She's alive?*

My relief was fleeting. Any minute now, I would see her again, only for her life to be stolen right in front of me. This was the Force's way of saying, *Look what happens when you disobey orders.*

"Her execution will proceed immediately." Commander Blank's voice broke slightly, and I realized that he didn't want Maelin to die either. He had dedicated eighteen months to shaping Maelin, Taig, Wick, Kanter, and me into guardians, and within twenty-four hours, he would lose three of us.

A Research unit emerged from another corridor, and among them was Ogga. He walked with that same, disgusting swing in his step, his chin held high. *To think I once looked up to him...*

I gritted my teeth and stepped forward, reaching for my bandolier. *I'll shoot a dart right through that phony pout of his.*

Kanter snatched my arm. His nails threatened to pierce through my overcoat sleeve as I pulled against him.

When Maelin followed the unit into the foyer, I finally stopped struggling, and Kanter released me.

It took a few seconds for Maelin's eyes to meet mine, and once they did, I could no longer hold myself together. My lips turned downward as I fought off tears. I heard her message loud and clear.

I'm passing the torch to you, Blimmery. Maelin smiled weakly. *Remember our deal, and use your words. Finish what I started.*

I flinched when an arrow struck her heart.

There was no countdown. No final words. I hadn't even realized that just seconds ago, a doctor had stepped onto a raised platform behind us, preparing his shot.

I screamed into my palm as I watched the life in Maelin's eyes fade. Surely the arrow had been laced with a fatal dose of calabar to ensure a near-instant kill. The Force had arranged this to portray themselves in a positive light, as if to say, *She deserves to suffer to the end, but we're showing her kindness by ending her misery.*

I refused to fall for the lie. Maelin didn't deserve a merciful death. She deserved no death at all.

The foyer exploded with shouts and sobs as Maelin fell, her rebellion against the Force ending with a few spastic attempts to get up.

Seeing her body suddenly still struck me like a physical blow. I staggered backward, accidentally stepping on two guardians' boots. They scolded me as I pivoted and shoved my way between them, forcing myself through the panicked crowd to reach the front door.

The sunrise greeted me outside, casting an orange glow across the distant burned remains of the commercial block.

I started the fire, and I got away with it.

I sprinted around the corner and hid in the same spot Taig and I had hidden the night before. My legs gave out, and my back slid down the stone wall until I was sitting on the grass, staring at the colorful morning clouds. After a few gasps for air, I leaned over and cried into my sweaty hands.

My head ached. My throat was parched. My lips were cracked. But despite the misery of my physical state, all I could focus on was how Maelin had died while I hadn't even received a slap on the wrist.

Footsteps approached me, followed by Kanter's voice.

"Blimmery."

I turned my head away from him, rubbing my face with my sleeves. Surely Kanter was here to announce that he had seen Maelin and me at Pandora's Ball, and that I had been acting strange all morning, and that I needed to come clean about everything. Even if I were to lie to him, he would see through my mask. He would turn me in, and the next execution would be mine.

It was strangely relieving—the thought of getting caught. I wouldn't have to live with this guilt. I *couldn't* live with this guilt.

Kanter sat beside me and took a deep breath. "You said that your cousin is a fan of Pandora's Box," he recalled. "So am I. Every event they host, I attend, but I never saw you at their balls, galleries, or plays. I never brought you to the archives."

With a sniffle, I looked him in the eye. He was offering to play ignorant, but I couldn't accept his charity.

"This is all my fault," I confessed. "Maelin and I, we—"

"Blimmery," he cut in.

"No, listen to me. Maelin and I both—"

"Stop. I don't wanna hear it."

"Kanter, we—"

"Quiet!"

I looked away from him again, tears falling faster than I could wipe them. *Please, don't make me do this alone. I'm not strong enough. To rid my chest of this weight, I must confess, but you're hanging me out to dry.*

Kanter reached for me, and I imagined a dagger in his hand. He would stab my chest like I deserved. Stab me like I stabbed Wick.

But there was no dagger. He simply wrapped his arm around me and gave my shoulder a pat. He was stiff, his body awkwardly far away. It was the worst comforting gesture I'd ever received, so bad that it made me chuckle through the tears. And I really needed that laugh.

"I know what it's like," Kanter whispered, "to be alone."

I stopped wiping my cheeks, allowing myself to sink into a fit of sobs. The first time, I cried for myself, but this time was for him.

How pitiful it is for a kind heart like Kanter to comfort a heartless creature like this.

About ten minutes after the execution, I was called to report immediately to the Investigation Office. I clung to the hope that a professor had reported me entering the archives with Kanter four days prior. *They finally suspect that I was involved in Maelin's obtaining of the Meridian book.*

But instead of a scolding or interrogation, the lead editor of *Capital Weekly* greeted me in the Office common room with an ear-to-ear smile.

"Doctor Delight!" he exclaimed, throwing his arms out. "I know it must be terribly sad to lose three fellow graduates, but we *really* need your optimism to clean this little mess of ours. And fast. Why don't you whip something up, and I'll get you a week off service to recoup?"

I was to write three cover-up articles. The first was for Maelin, to be published immediately. *The Belladonna Savior*, I titled it, gripping my pen so tightly that my wrist cramped up.

As the editor instructed, the story claimed she had aided a Defense unit on an expedition into the Atherus Empire. They traced the rebels who had looted one of our markets, and upon being found, the rebels attacked. Maelin died heroically in the crossfire.

"What will the Force think?" I asked when the editor approved my first draft. "We saw Maelin's execution. How could every guardian approve of us lying to the public like this?"

"Don't worry about that. We'll make it known that we're covering the truth to preserve morale. We must remain strong in the face of conflict to instill comfort and confidence in those we protect." He raised his brows with an open-mouth grin. "Oh, that was perfect! Add that to your internal notes."

The Force wrote this narrative to protect the hearts of Maelin's friends and family in Frontal and to avoid raising concerns about weakness within the Force, I jotted down, knowing that Maelin didn't even have friends and family in Frontal. *We must remain strong in the face of conflict to instill comfort and confidence in those we protect.* The internal notes would be filed with her article in the archives, only for guardians to lay their eyes upon.

Next, I wrote the second and third stories for Taig and Wick, which were to be published months apart. Sickness got the better of them, is what I settled on.

"Hmm... Why don't you make the Underground directly involved in Wick's death?" the editor suggested as he reviewed my first draft. "Two guardians dying of sickness might raise a brow here and there."

So I complied, crossing out the original line and replacing it with *An Underground rebel stabbed him.* There were no internal notes to be written. Taig's and Wick's articles would be filed in the death profiles, and while every guardian knew the truth about them now, that knowledge would fade with time. Someday, Taig Bitterview and Wick Saratoga would be nothing but names, lost in the archive's sea of paperwork.

The editor approved my revision with a chuckle, and sent me home with a golden ticket that read, *Respite Granted for the Preservation of Morale.*

Standing alone in my flat, the guilt of my uniform weighed me down. I had thought the day couldn't worsen, but now I had not only caused the death of three fellow graduates but had covered up my crimes. I had written stories to point the blame elsewhere, away from my hands.

I yanked my curtains shut to block out the morning light.

I got away with murder.

The brutal fact haunted me as I paced my flat. My head heated up. My chest was so tight I felt I had the weight of the entire island pressing upon my lungs. I was almost certain, for a moment, that I was drowning in poison, that someone had laced the air of my flat with toxins. It was relieving to think I could fall to the floor, and spare myself from the suffering I would forever endure.

My hand moved on its own, reaching for my dagger, but it was no longer in my overcoat. I had left it pierced in Wick's body. *I need to replace it, or the Force will find out.*

"No!" I argued, halting near my nightstand. I snatched my bedside lantern and chucked it across the room.

The lantern shattered upon impact, leaving a dent in the wall.

Let someone notice that I'm missing my dagger. Let them put the pieces together. Let them kill me!

I started pacing again, pondering my options. I could turn myself in. I could raise the question of how Taig had stabbed Wick, since Taig still had his dagger when the Force killed him. I could mention how there were three lock busters on the floor, not two. I could come clean to Kanter, despite his resistance, and let him serve me what he thought I deserved. I didn't know which route to take, but I had to do *something*, and fast.

Maelin's face appeared in my head, distracting me. She had trusted that I would improve the Force from within. What an awful job I was doing of it, to write her cover-up story immediately after they had shot her with that poisoned arrow. She had asked the wrong person for help. What she wanted of me was more than my worthless self could offer.

I'm sorry, Maelin. I'm a liar, after all. I can't fulfill your wish.

I reached for my dagger a second time, and once again, remembered that I no longer had it with me. I gritted my teeth and plucked a dart from my bandolier instead. *It's a smaller blade, but it'll do.*

With my back shoved against the wall, I aimed my dart downward, right above the edge of my armored vest.

This is the fastest way to right my wrong.

I closed my eyes, gripped the dart tighter, and pulled it away to prepare for a strike.

My hand froze mid-air, shaking as I tried to shove the blade into my chest.

Just do it already, I told myself, fighting the invisible force that tried to save me. *You're a writer, not a fighter. You can't handle pain, but you sure know how to cause it. So like the killer you are, just move that blade already!*

But the invisible force overpowered me. My arm didn't budge until I scoffed and chucked the dart away.

It pierced the wall, and I stormed toward it, shouting, "I'll kill you!"

My voice vanished into my flat, powerless. And for the second time that morning, tears fell, because I knew I couldn't do it. I didn't have what it would take. I was too weak to right my wrong, and too weak to live with the consequences. I was trapped in the horrible reality that I had dug three graves and had gotten away with it, and would forever carry this weight in my chest.

Through the blur of my tears, a rustic red notebook on my desk caught my attention. It was the one I had been writing my seventh iteration of *The Wallwalker* in, which, like usual, was nowhere near completion. My thoughts slowed, and in that brief moment of escape, I crept toward the notebook as though it were calling my name.

"I'm not a writer, Blimmery. I can't say things in a way that makes people listen."

My memory of Maelin's voice was so vivid that it felt as though she were right next to me, like her ghost had walked through the walls of my flat.

"But you know how to tell a good story. People all over the Empire read your articles."

When I sat at my desk, a beam of light slipped through a gap in my curtains, shining a golden spotlight on the notebook cover.

"You have more power than you believe."

I opened the notebook and began to tear out *The Wallwalker*, one page at a time. I cried over the loss of a story I loved—and I let it go.

You're a writer, not a fighter, I reminded myself, ripping a clump of pages from the spine. *To die would fix nothing. To die would mean running in fear, avoiding pain like you always do. So you're going to live with the pain, Blimmery, and you're going to do what you've never done before.*

I reached the first blank page and took a deep breath.

You're going to finish writing a book.

It would not be a classic Owding fantasy. It would not have a happy ending. It would not be what my family expected me to write, but what I *needed* to write.

I named my book of truth after Maelin, the girl who opened my eyes to evil. Without her, I would not know of darkness, but I would not work for light either. I would not have the strength to break down walls.

So I wielded my pen, and with my tears dotting the page, I wrote these words.

NIGHT SKY

If I could know for sure
that the sky is a giant graveyard
I might not grieve

If I could know
that each star is planted there
for someone who died young
I might not mourn so much

I once knew a young girl
with short, curly locks
who died one summer
with purple ribbons in her hair

I want to watch the night sky
and remember them

I want to say, *There, that one is Shanna*
She had the bluest eyes
And see, that bright, shiny one's for Jesse
He never cried

It is enough that their dreams were never finished
Why should they be forgotten too?

Life must offer some sweets
to those of us who live on
and remember

JENNIFER, AGE TWELVE

THE YEAR OF HER PASSING

ABOUT THE DEDICATION

Jennifer was such a positive force. While she expressed her fears in writing, she never talked about them openly. I have a feeling she understood people's concern for her health and made it her mission to lift their spirits. Even during painful hospital procedures, she would always smile and plot her next practical joke to make the nurses laugh.

I have never met anyone quite like her.

THOMAS CLARK

JENNIFER'S UNCLE - MAY 13, 2023

Get Lost. in bonus content for
Maelin

Explore deleted scenes, author interviews, artwork, and more

LOSTISLANDPRESS.COM

ACKNOWLEDGMENTS

Thank you Mom, Dad, and John, for the unwavering support of my books over the years.

Angie Eggers, for being my Cove. Younger me sometimes claimed we were cousins instead of friends because it felt more like the truth.

Joy Kabigting, for the adventure of a lifetime. What a coming-of-age story it was to enter adulthood together.

Non Wannapa Lisa and Ploy Lungkham, for the amazing friendship. I can't imagine my life without you two.

Sebastian Delgado, for you-know-what. You didn't know I knew, but now you know, I know. So I guess we both know.

Katie Flanagan, for working on projects with me since the budding days at Lost Island Press, and for editing this novella.

Natasha Orsh, for the gorgeous cover illustration.

My beta readers, for providing constructive criticism on an early draft. Without your help, *Maelin* wouldn't be the tale it is today:

> S. J. Robert, Ayaan Chowdhury, Concha Alvarez, Hessa, Arham Chowdhury, Kai Sao I., Abigail Lavery, Eden Rosewood, Germaine Han, Martine Alexandra Hassel Baardseth, Sarthak Aman, Victoria Nunweiller, Elaine Moraa, Amanda Lauren, A. S. H., Shawn McKeegan, Anaïs Lowe, Chi Mary, Víctor Cantelar Sagrado, Isobel McNeill, Nitya Mattey, Mads M., Taki M, Fox Gardner, Laurel Glyn, Ariya Bandy, Millie Bass, Ananya Bhai, Luis Rodrigues

Once again, sending my love to Grandpa Pete. *I will write another, and another, and another...*

Finally, thank *you*, for sparing a brief moment of your life to explore this little world of mine.

NIGHTSHADE ACADEMY

BELLADONNA, BOOK 1

Twenty teenagers are selected for an elite military boarding
school, but only five will emerge as guardians—destined for
a life of glamour and brutality.

CAPSULE

When a menacing app called Capsule auto-installs onto
Jackie's phone, she enters a game interlaced with reality
—a game threatening to kill.

LEAVING WISHVILLE

Ten years after his father's disappearance, Benji plans to
escape from his self-isolated coastal town—but leaving
Wishville may cost him his life.

ABOUT THE AUTHOR

MEL TORREFRANCA is a full-time author and founder of Lost Island Press. Her books feature morally gray characters, bold endings, and a pinch of awkward humor. Mel discovered her passion for writing at the age of seven and published her debut novel, *Leaving Wishville*, during high school. She also drinks way too many lattes.

MELTORREFRANCA.COM

ABOUT THE PUBLISHER

LOST ISLAND PRESS publishes dystopian, sci-fi, and fantasy books. Unlike mainstream presses, we don't publish everything for everyone. We publish for *you*. Our catalog offers grounded, character-driven stories that linger long after the last page. The kind you get lost in, that keep you up at night. And because our books have the same vibe, if you enjoy one, you'll enjoy them all.

LOSTISLANDPRESS.COM

Join our newsletter to claim a free ebook

www.ingramcontent.com/pod-product-compliance
Lightning Source LLC
Chambersburg PA
CBHW021552310726
48972CB00003B/790